Delaney's People

Beth Duke

ISBN-13:978-0615568447
(The Art of Dixie)
ISBN-10:0615568440

For Lucile, Patricia and Savannah:
possessors of great beauty and sparkle

CONTENTS

Acknowledgments

Thank you, God.

I am lucky to have many jewels in my life—every single member of my family and some very dear friends. I can't possibly name them all here.

Thanks to my wonderful daughter Savannah, who read two wildly disparate short stories and challenged me to tie them together. A book was born.

There are people who loved me enough to encourage and cheerlead me through this whole process. My sweet and beautiful first readers include Lillian Pizzo, Debbie Tuckerman, Marianne Barnebey, Kris Gause, Marietta Sophie Loudon, Eime Owens and *most especially* Beth Monette and Lucinda Hathaway. They endured every rewrite with great enthusiasm and patience.

Of course I thank my mother, Patricia Poucher, and my grandmother, Lucile Kadle Holder Sodeman . . . the two of you inspired me and made me keep writing. You still do.

My Cousin Debi Carnaroli, Uncle Reese Holder and Other Mother JoAnne Duke told me my stories were good, and I've always believed everything any of them has said.

Dad, if it weren't for the lessons in perseverance, the book might not be in print. Thank you, Bob Poucher.

Chris Bohjalian, Rick Bragg and Joshilyn Jackson provided encouragement and motivation, each in their unique way. I am deeply grateful.

Crystal McCartney of Carrollton, Georgia got the first draft of my manuscript printed in record time, with a smile.

Authors are thieves. Though this book is entirely fiction, I may have borrowed an image or two from someone and built a character or scene around it. If that is you, I am indebted.

Jay, Jason and Savannah—you make my Alabama skies even bluer, every single day. Nothing great could be anything without getting to share it with you.

Jewels

Margaret—2006

There are diamonds in the red clay of northeast Alabama. Delaney is one of them.

She is my great-granddaughter. On Wednesdays, her mother brings her by after her Toddler Tumble class. Delaney sits on my lap and pats my necklace.

She never pulls, twists, or tries to eat my various necklaces—she just pats them delicately with her tiny dimpled hand like soft moonlight whispering over the pearls. She seems to love faceted crystal beads and rhinestones in particular.

Delaney is my grandson Tommy's daughter, and so much like him I'm convinced his wife Lisa was just an incubator. Her hair is a soft cloud of curly golden ringlets, and her huge brown eyes crinkle like his when she laughs. She laughs often, like the Irish ancestors whose name she bears. She smells like Cheerios and baby soap.

When she comes to Arlington Shores, my neighbors envy my

thirty minutes of joy. Gloria Ledbetter peeks through her curtains to glare when they arrive, Mr. Henderson always greets them from his tiny front porch, and Bitsy Miller will wave if she's out walking. Most of us think that a retirement community probably shouldn't share its name with the best-known cemetery in the country. We like it here, but the running joke is that they come and attach a headstone to your condo door when your time's up, as in, "Arlington Snores."

As Delaney pats my jewelry, I am transported to the time when I first wore it long ago. I may not have been Babe Paley, but in my day, I spent lots of time and even more money at Gelfman's Department Store on chic clothes and the latest costume jewelry. My collection includes pieces by Haskell, Hobé, Trifari . . . there's over sixty years' worth of jewelry in my closet, and all of it has a memory or two attached.

The first time Lisa brought Delaney over I was wearing my triple strand of faux pearls with the rhinestone spacers and my periwinkle dress, as I had been to my weekly old lady bridge game. Delaney really likes that one, because sometimes it creates rainbows on the wall. I bought it in 1952 and wore it with an elegant black shirtwaist to Darrell's fundraising dinner when he ran for state senate. He never came close to winning, but I looked fabulous at that event. Somewhere, there's a newspaper clipping that shows Darrell, me, Carolyn and Dennis Tharpe, and Julia Neece with her husband. We'd had a lot of wine that night, and my arm was resting lightly on Darrell's shoulder. He was leaning forward and ever so slightly toward Carolyn. I didn't know at the time that he was leaning a lot more toward her at the office. We looked shiny, polished and new, so young and happy in our world.

Another of Delaney's favorites is the citrus Miriam Haskell bead torque. In 1940, we spent our first year on Cottonwood Avenue, in the only house Darrell and I ever owned. It was the one where I baked endless cookies, where I rolled bandages a few years later for WWII, where I kissed boo-boos and sat up all night with Ellen because she had the croup. When she pats that one, I see myself spending twenty dollars for it at a time when that was a month's groceries. I loved it too much to pass it up, though, and Darrell's practice was doing well.

When Ellen was born, Darrell gave me the most exquisite McClelland Barclay sterling silver choker—a vine with a dangling floral design. I wore it constantly, and when Ellie was teething, I let her clamp down on a flower now and then. The tiny teeth marks are still there, and I treasure it as much for that as for anything else. Delaney adores her Grandma Ellen, and I've tried to explain that she made those marks as a baby years ago. I don't think she quite believes me, though. Grandma Ellen has always been sixty with silver hair in her mind, though she once had Tommy and Delaney's golden ringlets. The sixty part might be right, however, as my little Ellie was a serious and brilliant infant. She was speaking in complete sentences at one and a half, knew her alphabet before she was two, and regularly settled arguments among her less mature playmates.

She examines a brass kaleidoscope my father gave me for my twelfth birthday. A Limoges Eiffel Tower Darrell bought me in Paris, and then a silver filigree music box from Ellen. Delaney gazes intently at them, poised with her arms folded carefully behind her back. She leans forward, looking remarkably like Foghorn Leghorn as she explores my étagère. I'll give Lisa credit for that, thanks to her gentle suggestion, "We don't touch Mama D's pretty things." Lisa is one of those modern mothers whose lips are incapable of forming the word "no." I imagine her saying, "Now, Delaney, let's take our fingers out of the electrical socket and color instead."

Fortunately, my great-granddaughter is a naturally well-behaved child. If Lisa has another, she may find "No!" a bit more acceptable. We'll see.

I take the kaleidoscope down, and let Delaney squinch her eye to look inside. She's every bit as captivated by the colors, patterns and sparkles as I am. It's the reason she shares my love for the brilliant rhinestones and rainbows in my jewelry. We can "ooh" and "ahh" together for hours, this child and I.

Delaney doesn't know it yet, but she's exceptionally beautiful. Really—that's not idle great-grandmother talk. Lisa is threatening to put her in one of those insipid baby beauty pageants, and though I don't comment, I pray she doesn't. Not commenting is the hardest part of being ninety years old and watching the mistakes your progeny makes. Everyone thinks old people don't have opinions, but we do. We know enough to keep them to ourselves most of the time. For instance, when Lisa wears her green floral Capri pants, or when she puts those huge, fluffy socks on poor Delaney that make her look like a tottering Clydesdale.

My great-granddaughter is very talkative while she's in my lap today, and I suspect Lisa has told her nice things to say to Mama D. Where else would she get the idea to ask how I'm feeling, and if I enjoyed my bridge game? Toddlers don't talk that way, and I prefer when she lets Delaney say whatever's on her mind. Usually, that's whether there's ice cream in my freezer or if I know that her puppy "still pee pees in the living room sometimes." She used to think there could be a monster under her bed, but it was "my abernation." Mickey Mouse is definitely not just her abernation, because she has seen him, and he's real. And, most solemnly, Delaney plans to wear "big girl pennies" very soon. Her mommy bought them in pink because that's her favorite color except for purple.

I remember a sparkling pink and lavender rhinestone Schiaparelli parure—that was for Mrs. McKenzie's 100th birthday luncheon. I wore it with a very smart knit suit in cream. You should have seen Delaney's eyes light up when she saw that glittering jewelry! On that day, everything got patted—the bracelet, the brooch, the earrings, and of course the necklace. It was my most extravagant jewelry purchase ever, but a lady deserves something very special for inspiration when she's starting a new life. I didn't think Darrell should get to skimp on my final charge to our account at Gelfman's.

I was standing in the kitchen packing Ellen's lunch when the call came. At first, I thought she had the wrong number, because she simply couldn't be looking for me. I even told her she was looking for a different Margaret Parker, though there weren't any others in our town. How do you respond when an anonymous woman calls to tell you that your husband is having an affair with his secretary? For the first fifteen minutes, I thought it must be some kind of joke. I hung up the phone, finished making the peanut butter and jelly sandwich, and calmly drove Ellie to school. I sat there, numb, in the parking lot, reliving a hundred little moments when I should have known. The next minute, I'd be convinced that this nightmare was someone else's. It was a mistake. It was a mix-up. Darrell would explain it; Darrell could always explain everything.

Then I remembered his secretary Carolyn's new rhinestone bracelet, the one she'd shown me the previous week. It caught my eye as soon as I saw her arm, so naturally, I took a closer look.

"Oh, it's just paste, Margaret—you know I could never afford such a thing on my salary!" she exclaimed.

I found that curious.

It was unbelievably brilliant, so much so that I couldn't help but ask, "Where did you find such a treasure?"

She replied, "I really can't remember. I'm not even sure what store it was."

In retrospect, she was downright consumed with the work on her desk that day, and didn't seem to want to chat. Suddenly, I had a terrible suspicion about Carolyn's jewelry. I raced home, dug through my husband's oh-so-orderly desk, and found the truth under a black plastic drawer tray: a receipt from Couch's Jewelers for a diamond bracelet.

I don't own a diamond bracelet. I made my usual trip to the grocery store, bought three cans of slimy oysters, and then emptied them carefully into the space beneath the spare tire in Darrell's beloved new Buick.

Had I ever really believed he needed to work late four nights a week? Could any woman be more stupid, more delusional, more betrayed? I sobbed as I choked down my cruel and jagged new stereotype. I had been the smiling wife of a successful attorney, a devoted mother, the First Vice-President of the Junior League. I was the last to know, the first to cry, the first to want to bludgeon. I removed a dark pin from my hair and twisted it around in the trunk lock until it broke off clean. *Here's my heart, Darrell.*

I drove home and packed my husband's clothes, a few of his least favorite things, and a note saying that he didn't live in our house anymore. The boxes were waiting for him on the front porch when he got home that night. Ellie and I were at my mother's house.

The next few years were the hardest of my life. Ellen and I fought a lot, but I made allowances because I knew how much she missed her father. I waited a long time to tell Ellie what he'd done because I couldn't cause her any more pain. I took the blame for our divorce until I decided one day I could no longer bear her silence, her surliness, and the weight of her accusation. Eventually, she forgave her father. I never did.

Occasionally, I let Delaney try on a Trifari necklace I bought in the fifties. It has deep blue glass beads with tiny green flower accents. I wore it on my first day as a sales clerk at Gelfman's jewelry counter. It always brought me luck, and eventually, it brought me a handsome man named Carl when he told me it matched my eyes. We were married for thirty-seven years. His absence is still a constant presence, but it only whispers to me now, and I don't cry.

Carl was one of those men you see in commercials, the kind who illustrate how men age beautifully and women don't. At fifty, he already had a lot of gray in his brown hair, and the most dazzling smile that gathered the wrinkles beside his deep brown eyes. His wife died two years before I met him, of some sort of cancer. The poor man had successfully resisted the attempts his friends made to introduce a new romance. He came into Gelfman's to buy a birthday present for his niece, Angela, and I sold him a perfect sparkling

Monet bracelet with tiny cherubs around it. He left with my phone number and our future woven together in his mind. That's what he told the guests at our wedding.

Delaney will never fully understand how she brought light and joy back into my life after Carl died. What rapture I felt the first time I touched her tiny face, and watched her fingers curl around mine. She is my future, the hopes and dreams of a very old lady.

My will is very clear—my jewelry goes to my great-granddaughter, and she is to keep and enjoy it. I hope Delaney wears her favorites from time to time. I hope I get to accompany her to her prom in the form of my Weiss rhinestone choker. I hope she wears my pearls at her wedding. I hope her daughter likes to pat every single bit of it, and feels the love I left behind.

A Diamond
Sam—1916

My father-in-law, his father Patrick and I sat in the rocking chairs on the front porch. The women carried piles of bloody sheets and cloth out the front door, sweat dripping from their faces in the July heat. Each smiled at us reassuringly, but I was certain that my Nancy could not possibly be alive.

Doc Phillips had been in there since ten o'clock last night. His motorcar was parked next to my barn full of mules, a shiny black pestilence that scattered the screaming chickens when he roared up.

"She's all right, son," Jack Delaney offered, eyes firmly fixed on mine. I was afraid he was going to ask me to pray with him again, and I didn't have the strength to do it. All I wanted in this world was to know that my wife and son were healthy. Nancy had stopped screaming hours ago. More recently, her sister Eula offered a terse, "Mother and baby are all right, Sam. You should get some rest."

I could no more relax at this point than chew a hole through the wooden boards under me.

"Your nerves are shot, boy," Patrick smiled at me. "How about we have a drink to celebrate the new baby? A toast to wee Patrick?"

Nancy's Irish grandfather never missed a chance to drink whiskey, in celebration or melancholy. It might be eleven o'clock in the morning, but his ancient internal monitor was telling him a drop was required to get through whatever the rest of this day might bring.

"Let's wait for Doc Phillips, Patrick," I said, though I could have used something to steady my shaking hands. I looked at my worn old black boots, and thought about what it would mean to have a son to help me in the fields. Our older daughter, Esther, had a back as strong as any boy in Cleburne County. Her little sister Deirdre had her head in the clouds most days. I suppose at six she was still entitled to spend more time daydreaming than working on her chores. Nancy said so, but she was awfully soft on the girls. They were at Mrs. Wilson's down the road. I was grateful they had been spared the night of worry over their mother.

The screen door groaned suddenly, and I glanced up expecting to see more linens being toted out to the wash tub. Arthur Phillips was smoothing his white hair back from his wrinkled forehead, hat and bag in his spotted left hand. "Gentlemen, Nancy and the babe are doing all right. Sam, I would like to speak with you privately. Would you walk me out to my car?"

"Your wife has been through quite an ordeal, Sam," he began, looking to the cloudless blue sky as if for divine inspiration. "She lost a right lot of blood last night, but she will recover. The thing is, Sam, her woman parts are never going to allow her to bear another child. Do you understand what I am telling you, son?"

"I think I do, Doc. We have been blessed with two daughters and a son. I cannot ask the Lord for more than that, can I?" I smiled briefly into the old man's eyes, trying to determine if this was his way of telling me that I could never have relations with my wife again.

"Not exactly, Sam." He stopped and kicked the tire at the rear of his Ford, hard enough to shake the car a bit. "Your new baby is a fine, beautiful daughter. Nancy wanted me to be the one to tell you."

"A girl?" I was rendered speechless for a minute. Suddenly the idea of getting into Doc's motorcar and riding away with him seemed like a good idea. I would rather do that than face Nancy's disappointment and try to hide my own. "We were sure this time. Mrs. Hawkins told Nancy two months ago she was carrying a boy, without a doubt. She did some sort of test on her that never fails."

Doc looked back at the sky, as if I were trying his medical patience mightily with the midwife's foolishness. "Well Sam, those so-called tests are not very reliable. I am sorry you didn't get the son you wanted, but take this child from God and love her with all your heart. She is as pretty a baby as I have ever seen, and I have held a good many. Go be with them now. Nancy is waiting for you." With that he patted my back and walked around to the front of the shiny Ford to turn the crank over and over. Nothing happened, and for the thousandth time I wondered why a man would suffer the aggravation of these toys when a fine horse could provide reliable transportation and companionship, too. Finally the engine sputtered to life, scattering the hens once more. Doc waved goodbye as he bounced down our rutted clay driveway.

I remembered that instant that my horse—a chestnut Tennessee Walker named Thunder—was gone forever. Nancy didn't know yet, but I traded him a week ago for something dear. My sister Carrie would be long in forgiving me for parting with our father's prize stallion. I dreaded telling her, and decided it could wait until she visited from Savannah in two months. I'd have to write and tell her to bring trinkets for another niece—nothing blue.

I trudged back to the porch, Patrick and Jack eying me like I was a bedraggled stranger picking my way through the chickens, not the family member they had counted on for near nine years to take care of Nancy and everyone else who came running when times were hard. I straightened up and tried to look joyful. I reckoned joyful was what they were expecting from me, and I didn't want to let them down.

"Doc says Nancy is going to be on her feet soon, and we have a beautiful baby daughter," I smiled. "I'm going to go in and see them, and y'all can come on in a few minutes, all right?

Patrick and Jack glanced at each other quickly, a Sunday sermon of unspoken words between them, then nodded to me in unison. Old Pat brushed off his pants and muttered quietly, "I believe I'll look for that drink."

Nancy was propped up on the rose-print pillows. I could see she was making an effort to hide that she had been crying, though the dark red and green splotches amid the lighter flowers gave her away. "I want to call her Margaret," she offered, her gaze vaguely directed toward the tiny wood cradle.

"Margaret is a fine name, Nan."

I could see her shoulders starting to shake. "Sam . . . the doctor said . . ."

"Hush, Sweet Nan. We will talk about this later. Let me see if this girl is as pretty as her mama." I reached into the cradle and picked up the tiny bundle, trying not to awaken it and bring on more female hysteria. She was a lovely thing, all right—dark hair peeked out from her white cap, and she had long brown eyelashes that did not seem possible on a newborn babe. She squirmed under all the swaddling the women used to encase her body. I wondered if they knew it was nearly one hundred degrees outside, but thought better than to question their methods.

As if on cue, Eula appeared in the doorway. Nancy's sister had the most annoying way of intruding on any moment people shared privately. I'd been wishing for years she would get a husband and move out of her weary father's house, but Eula was not blessed overmuch in the looks department. She was gloomy and bitter, and her tongue was sharp enough to slice an onion. Her breath usually smelled like she had done just that. All we could do was hope that some poor half-blind boy might take a shine to her figure, which was slender and about all she had to offer.

"Sam, is it all right if I tell Daddy and Papa to come in now?" she asked. I would have liked a few more minutes alone with my wife and this Margaret in a soft pink wrapper, but I knew we had all shared a rough night and I needed to be gracious and let folks get home. If Patrick were left too long with my corn whiskey, he'd be sleeping on the sofa in the parlor before I could stop him.

"Of course, Eula," I smiled and gently swung the bundle back and forth. Nancy looked out the bedroom's only window, searching for words to offer the Delaney males.

My wife held out her skinny arms, gesturing for me to place the baby there. As her father and grandfather walked in, she put on a brave smile and nodded. I knew she was missing her mother and grandmother—it didn't seem right having to share this moment with only men. My heart wrenched at the new thought: I would never have a son to carry on the Dawson name.

Patrick was spry for an old man; his big frame carried two hundred pounds and I figured he could still beat a fellow twenty years his junior. He reached out and took my new daughter from Nancy, hugging her to his massive chest. "Ah, Nancy girl, your Margaret is a beauty like her own mother." He pulled at the layers of cloth, trying to get some air to the poor thing. The women would have fussed, but I was on his side.

The baby started to wake. Instead of handing her back, Patrick continued his exploration, fixated on Margaret's neck. "What's this?" he squinted, one white eyebrow raised. "I think it's a wee birthmark." He froze, staring hard. "Aww, it can't be. But it is." I was amazed to see a tear running down the old man's cheek, tracing a wrinkle to his whiskered chin. He handed Margaret back to Nancy, awkwardly rubbing his face with the back of his arm.

"What's wrong, Papa?" Nancy looked down at our daughter, still fighting her blanket prison but not making a sound. I decided I should let Jack have a moment, then take the men out so Nan could feed her.

Jack was watching his father carefully. Rather than take the baby, he said, "Nancy, I'll come back tomorrow when you've had a rest. I need to get your grandfather home."

Nancy was clearly wondering what had disturbed Patrick. She kept examining the baby and simply nodded at her father. They did not share a great deal of affection, and I was relieved when he offered to go.

When we reached the porch, Patrick said, "Sam, the babe has a wee red diamond on her neck. You don't know the story behind God's message to me, but I do. Your Margaret will have a blessed life." With that, he picked up his hat from the rocking chair and nodded to Jack.

"Wait a minute, Pat. What story?"

"Aww, 'tis nothing bad, Sam. Not to worry. Me mother Mary Kathleen made herself known to me today, that's all."

With that cryptic statement, he climbed down the stone steps and headed for Jack's wagon. My father-in-law offered, "He's an old man, Sam, but he lost his mother at an age to make her a saint in his mind. You know that. There's a legend dating back to his days in Ireland about a diamond, but I've never heard the whole thing. I'll get him a glass or two of whiskey later, and get it out of him."

I shrugged my shoulders and turned to find Eula standing in the doorway, silently scolding me the way women do to men everywhere. I had no idea what I'd done wrong, but I quickly decided to go feed our animals and give her time to leave.

After an eternity, Eula mounted her horse and headed toward home. I tiptoed back into the still house to find Nancy snoring softly, the pink bundle under her arm. I spotted a small red diamond shape behind the baby's left ear and stroked it gently with my thumb. Margaret turned her head toward it, still sound asleep.

My wife did not get a diamond ring when I asked her to marry me. Thunder was gone, but I had a small token to celebrate the birth of our new child. I slipped the velvet box under Nancy's pillow as she cradled our daughter, a tired smile on her lips.

God Loves Darrell
Darrell—1933

The young men were kings in this town, though their kingdom was desolate much of the time these days. Fortunate sons home from college—Vanderbilt University, no less—for summer at the height of the Great Depression. One will be in love by fall semester, and the other will be sentenced to stay at home, his father losing the last vestige of the income they'd thought would flow forever from the fabric mill.

The national mood had been lifted, slightly, along with Prohibition; so many sorrows to drown. It made no difference to these two, accustomed to the best white lightning in the county. They planned to meet Parsons, their bootlegger, at 12:15 a.m. out on Highway 7, briefly interrupting his weekly run to Birmingham.

First, though, they had this Saturday night: starry, breezy, mysterious, throbbing with young-man excitement. They were, improbably, hiding in a hay barn. They followed a girl, a newcomer, more exotic and beautiful than any they've seen here or in Nashville. Her hair was long and deep brown, almost black. Her eyes were huge and luminescent dark amber, and her skin was a perfect creamy light tan, as though she loved the sun. Her body? It was the reason the boys followed her discreetly in the moonlight, headlamps extinguished, for three miles from town. She and her friend—a lesser being—have settled on the front porch. Darrell wanted to watch her on the porch until they had to return to his car, hidden in the woods a hundred yards away. Parsons wouldn't wait, so they had to leave by midnight. They hoped to see into her bedroom window first.

She was walking arm and arm with her friend out of *King Kong*, at the appropriately named Princess Theatre. Darrell, used to picking young girls like ripe apples from his family's orchard, was rendered shy and cautious by her beauty. He said to Hoyt, "I am going to have this girl; she's my damn gift for two semesters of grueling study at Vandy." God loved him, always had.

They tried to figure out who her family is. The farm used to belong to the Ledbetters, but this is no Ledbetter. She was Maggie somebody. They heard that much from her friend. When she'd stepped onto the pink neon sidewalk after the movie, Maggie had on a thin cotton sweater. She removed it now with a shrug, fanning herself. It was getting hot on the porch. The young men prayed, "Please go to your bedroom, Maggie, and stand in the open window. Breathe the summer air into your beautiful lungs, wearing your sheer nightgown. We will watch faithfully."

Instead, Maggie shocked them both by stepping off the porch and walking toward the barn, furtively glancing back at the house. Did she know the boys were among the bales, peeking out? She stopped beside a tall snowball bush ten feet away and waited for her friend to join her, perfectly silhouetted in front of the orange moon. She shocked the boys and thrilled them a little, too, by removing a cigarette from her bosom and lighting it, her lovely face lit by its glow with each drag. Darrell turned to Hoyt in amazement—girls do not smoke. Certainly, ladies do not smoke. Did Maggie move here from Atlanta? Charleston? Her friend did not partake at first, but succumbed to what could only be her desperate wish to become Maggie-like. She coughed and sputtered, causing them both to dissolve into giggles. Inside the house, a light went on. The girls ground the cigarette butt into the dirt, then picked it up and hid it near the barn. They waved their arms frantically at the smoke hanging in the air. Finally, they decided it was a good time to go to bed. The boys know this because that's the one word they could make out—bed. They watched and waited, eager for Maggie to appear upstairs.

After ten minutes, the boys gave up. Wherever Maggie undressed, it's a place forbidden to their eyes. The house was dark, sound asleep. Darrell nudged Hoyt and told him, "It's time to meet Parsons."

Highway 7 was deserted save for a fat possum crossing to the other side of the forest. Darrell parked under a huge old oak tree, lights out, waiting for a sign. At 12:21 he finally got it: a car approached, flashing his lights twice. Darrell flashed back thrice and watched the car pass. He waited for Parsons to appear at his window, which he did suddenly, scaring him to death. Parsons was grinning, his greasy hair hanging in his face, three days of unshaven gray whiskers framing his two missing front teeth. After they concluded their business, Darrell and Hoyt headed home for a taste. They're diverted, however, by sirens and flashing lights racing around and ahead of them, cornering hard at Black Creek Road. They followed, curious.

It was hard to miss the fire—billowing yellow flames licking the smoky clouds in the sky. Darrell's heart sank and then rose: he stopped to help. When they pulled up, it was apparent that the hay barn was gone, but the house could be saved. Maggie's house. Darrell and Hoyt exited the car, looking for something heroic to do in the chaos. Because God loved Darrell and always had, he spotted a huge gray cat crouching in terror under a bush and swept it up, carrying it valiantly to Maggie, praying it was hers. She immediately began to cry. "Thank you so much for saving Matilda," she sobbed. Matilda tired quickly of being clutched in her arms and leaped, trailing black marks on Maggie's hands and white robe. She spread them to her beautiful face as she wiped a tear away.

Darrell seized the moment, introducing himself. She informed him, "My name is Margaret Dawson." He is so very sorry about the fire, and glad he could stop to help. He stood with Maggie-turned-Margaret, solemnly watching the firemen fight the blazes down to a manageable size, then turned to her and said, "Good night, I have to get home." His parents would be worried. Maybe he could see her in town sometime. Does she ever go to the movies?

Her father lets her use his Oldsmobile sometimes, a rare thing indeed for a girl in 1933. He must dote on her, but allow her more than the usual freedom, as well. Darrell asked, "Can I meet you there next Saturday, to see *Queen Christina*?"

Margaret said, "I'll try," smiling at Darrell briefly. Her parents stood in their nightclothes two feet away. She turned to them and they held each other and watched the last of the fire; a bit of hay was still burning in a little pile.

The following Saturday, Darrell fetched Hoyt at 6:00, determined to stake out the best place to spot Margaret. Much to his surprise, she was dropped off by her mother, no doubt to get picked up later. But she was alone, Karen-less. Hoyt, rendered useless, decided to walk home.

She greeted Darrell with a brilliant smile and linked her arm with his. When they were seated, the conversation was awkward. She told him, "I appreciated the help you and Hoyt gave us with the fire, especially when I'd been so worried about poor Matilda. My father is planning to rebuild as soon as he can get the lumber." She stared at her hands then, looking lost in thought.

So he whispered, "Do they know how the fire started?"

"They're not sure," she replied, examining her hands more closely. She told Darrell, "It was a big loss for my father, and he can't afford another big loss." They were going from dirt poor to rock poor fast. Then she bewildered Darrell by crying. He slid his arm around her shoulders as the lights went down.

While Greta Garbo flickered on the screen, a plan arranged itself in his mind. He will explain to Mr. Dawson that he was driving to meet a friend late last Saturday night and tossed a cigarette out his window, utterly carelessly, as he passed their farm. He hadn't thought about it, but when his daughter told him they weren't sure how the fire started, he realized the truth. He would express his deepest sincere apology, and pay to rebuild the barn better than before and stock it with hay.

The last part would not be that difficult. Judge Parker appreciated his eldest son's taking responsibility like a man. There would be harsh words and recriminations, but ultimately there would be lumber from their sawmill and whatever else Darrell needed to make this right. He'd tell his father he'd do most of the labor himself, though he planned to get Hoyt and a few other guys to chip in if possible. He imagined Margaret bringing him iced tea and sandwiches for lunch. It was an elegant solution. The real truth was known only to Margaret, Karen, Hoyt and Matilda the barn cat. He was pretty sure none of them would talk.

When the movie ended, his arm was exactly where he placed it, warm and reassuring. He stood and offered his hand to help her up, pulling a bit too hard, drawing her close and clasping her hand to his chest, holding it over his heart. She looked up and smiled, embarrassed but not moving away. Darrell asked, "Will your mother be waiting?" She nodded her head yes. When they walked out, blinking to adjust their eyes, the tattered Oldsmobile was already in front. Darrell opened the passenger door for Margaret, then ran around to speak with Mrs. Dawson. "I need to talk with your husband about an important matter," he said, "and I'll drive out after church, if that's all right."

When he arrived, still slicked up in his Sunday best, Mr. Dawson was waiting on the front porch in holey bib overalls with iced tea in hand. He stood to greet Darrell, but offered him none; he gestured to the stiff wood chair placed four feet away, already arranged to face him. Margaret and her mother were nowhere in sight.

Darrell hesitated for the briefest of seconds, then began his carefully rehearsed speech. The older man watched him intently, the lines in his face becoming deeper furrows with each sentence. Darrell rushed a bit to the climax, "I'll build you a new barn, Mr. Dawson, painted as you choose, full of the best alfalfa hay in time for winter. Of course, I'll replace whatever else was lost in the fire; all I need is a list. I will start getting things together tomorrow; and I can begin construction as early as Wednesday. I am so very sorry for what I've done. It was just downright stupid." Darrell forced himself to stop talking. Margaret's father was staring at the worn floorboards on the porch, his sweaty tea glass dripping between his clasped hands.

Mr. Dawson sat very still for what seemed like forever. He moved only to set the tea down, never once looking up, his gnarled hands resting on his knees. Darrell willed himself to remain silent. Finally, he stood and extended his hand to Darrell, announcing, "I reckon that will be fair. I had some tools in that barn, too, and Mrs. Dawson will have it all written down for you tomorrow morning at seven o'clock." He turned and entered the house without another word, his tea glass sitting in a puddle of sweat next to his chair. Darrell is summarily dismissed in silence, the creaky screen door in his face.

The work went smoothly, and Mr. Dawson was pleased with his new barn and seventy dollars' worth of new tools. Darrell was disappointed by Margaret's failure to appear each day; he only glimpsed her now and then, though she did offer him lemonade on the hottest days. He learned pretty quickly that he needed to head home for lunch. He was in the habit of stripping to his white undershirt as the day heated up, hoping she noticed his tanned muscles beneath. He cultivated a pencil-thin mustache, fancying himself Clark Gable-like. All of this yielded no more than five glasses of lemonade, though he thought Margaret spied on him from a window upstairs a time or two.

One day he borrowed a company truck to pick up hay, and he

asked Mr. Dawson, "May Margaret might ride along with me?"

The old man stomped a clod of red clay off his boot, then stared off into the distance. Finally he pronounced two words, "All right."

"So, you're about done," Margaret yelled, trying to make him hear above the roar of the truck. He grinned and cupped his hand to his ear, eyebrows raised. Then he patted the seat next to him in suggestion. She slid over, eyes on the windshield. "I said, you're about done."

"With the barn, yes. With you, no."

Margaret blushed. He reached for her hand, clasping it again to his chest.

"Do you think your father will let you go to Rainbow Beach tomorrow?"

"What is Rainbow Beach?"

"It is the finest beach in the landlocked portion of Alabama. It's really a big lake, with tons of sand trucked in. You can swim, and there's a diving platform out in the lake. It's just like the real thing, only without seashells. And waves. Unless a fat guy does a cannonball."

"Sounds heavenly. Do you go there a lot?"

"No, I haven't been this summer. I figure I deserve a reward, though. I've worked hard to repay your daddy." He released her hand, swerving a little to avoid a turtle in the road. When he reached to take it back, it's clasped in her lap, the object of sudden, absorbing fascination.

"You know, Darrell, I wanted to talk to you about that. I just don't know where to begin. I . . . ."

". . . was smoking and started a fire? We saw you out there that night, Margaret. I told you I drove by."

She turned in the seat to regard his face. "You knew?"

He tells her, "I suspected, not knew. Your secret will always be safe, locked away," he clasped her hand to his chest once more, "here."

No more was discussed about the fire, for whatever reason. Maybe Margaret chose to believe Darrell also threw a cigarette in the barn's direction. Neither of them revisited the subject for years to come. There was the rest of the summer, and it held a lot of promise.

The next morning, Darrell arrived to pick Margaret up at ten o'clock. She came to the door with a big picnic basket. Her mother, standing behind her, wished them "fun at the beach". Margaret wore a plain blue dress, which he hoped was covering a swimsuit.

And it was—kelly green, with a flouncy little skirt trimmed in white lace. The straps were narrow, edged in white also, and its bust line was cut deep enough to let Darrell know he was dating a goddess. He was mesmerized.

They went to the "beach" a lot that summer; a few movies, and a birthday party for Hoyt. One night, Hoyt confided to Darrell over moonshine, "The mill has laid off almost all its workers, and I'm expected to pitch in. I won't be back at Vanderbilt anytime soon, buddy."

Truth was, he never returned, and they both suspected it at the time.

It was August-hot on the black leather back seat of Judge Parker's Packard that last night, and Darrell slowly licked a tiny bead of sweat from behind Margaret's ear. She smelled like vanilla.

"Wait for me. I'll be back at Thanksgiving," he murmured into her neck.

"I will," she replied.

He felt sure about it. God loved him, and always had.

In the Heat of the Moment
Mr. Sam Dawson—1953

As I was nearing the end of my life, I had to write down a secret that I was never able to share with a soul. Always was between me and Jesus, and still it haunted me for nearly twenty years. My wife, Nancy, would wake me in cold sweats, shaking like a poisoned dog. I hope and pray I am forgiven before I go to meet the Lord. He knows what is in my heart, and why I did what I did.

My lovely bride was raised in comfort. Her daddy was a wealthy man, good and fair, too. He lived to be eighty-eight years old, but long before he passed on, he shared his fortune with his children. His son, Jacob, ran the stables; daughters Eula and Nancy and their husbands were each given fifty percent of the Delaney Store, which eventually became the Cleburne Gulf Service Station and General Store. I never heard it called anything but the short name, though. The older Delaney boy, James, died in WWI, The Great War.

Nancy and I had been married for a long time when Eula met Sly MacDonald, and I knew from the start he was trouble. When they joined us in the store, we all got along pretty good, I guess, but Sly had a habit of going off and laying up drunk for a day or two here and there. No one told the old man; they loved him, didn't want to upset him, and Eula covered his tracks pretty well.

This went on for years and damn years, and later, every one of us covered for Sly. I resented it. When Jack Delaney finally went to his reward, he left the family a bit of money. It was early 1930, and we didn't know enough to panic over the depression yet. Still, Nancy and I tucked our money away. Not in a bank, either.

In 1932, we offered to let Sly and Eula buy our portion of the store, and they thought it was a sensible thing to do with their inheritance. They changed their minds about that real quick, and things were never quite the same between Eula and Nancy afterward. Nancy and I moved with Margaret, the last of our children at home, to a farm nearer to town. We wanted her to have a good education, and maybe even go off to college someday. Nancy and I always encouraged our girls to learn, and to become teachers or nurses or other female-type professionals. Turns out, the only one who didn't get to be an educated working woman was Margaret, the one we toted off to a better school. It worked out all right for her, though.

Some months after we bought the Ledbetter place, Sly turned up on my front porch looking like the devil, whiskey flashing in his eyes. He grumbled, "I wanna to talk to you private-like." We went off to the barn. He started in telling me all this mess about, "I know you been stealin' from the store's cash register for years, and I'm gonna prove it. I want you to give me a hundred dollars, right now."

"Sly," I said, "I never stole a damn thing, and you can go to hell." I figured he'd forget about it when he sobered up. I walked the damn fool out to his truck, and made sure he was pointed toward home before he drove off drunk. I forgot about it at the time. I never even told Nancy he'd come around, or what he said. Times were hard, and it seemed like the whole world was irritated to be alive some days. I figured old Sly was only feelin' the pressure, like the rest of us.

I was wrong, and it cost me dearly. One Saturday that summer, Nancy and Margaret went to town and left me working in the barn. I looked up, and there was Sly in the doorway, framed in sunlight. He was a little man, thin and wiry, and he seemed to get smaller every time I saw him. I never did figure out why I didn't hear his truck that day.

He started in on me again, saying, "You stole from me." This time, he'd had more than a few belts, and he said, "I'll march right into your house and tell Nancy and my purty little niece Maggie." There was something about the way he said that that flew all over me. I grabbed a shovel and started toward the yard, pushing him aside and telling him, "Get the hell off my property." I heard the click when he cocked his pistol, and turned back around.

"Now Sly," I told him, "put that away before you do some damn fool thing with it."

And he did, reaching into his pocket and producing a wad of dirty paper instead. "Get back in the barn, Sam," he told me, "I got somethin' to show you."

When I stepped inside, he started laying out all these pieces of paper, receipts he'd doctored to make it look like I'd shorted the register. I said, "No one in his right mind would believe I stole anything," and he answered, "Sheriff Owens sure might." He was going to take this "evidence" right over to him this very afternoon, if I didn't give him his due—*two* hundred dollars—immediately.

I told him, "Sly, you can shove your damned evidence, and I'll take my chances with the sheriff." It might have been fine then, if the fool had turned and left. Instead, he pulled that pistol out again and pointed it right at me. A man with a pistol pointed at you, brother-in-law or not, gets your attention real quick. A drunken, desperate man doing that requires some kind of action, and fast. I swung that shovel as hard as I could at his head, scattering his papers—now my evidence—all over the hay bales. He crumpled slowly, dropping the pistol with a loud thump. A river of blood flowed from his left ear, pressed to the floor.

Sly was dead. I had killed a man, and I can still replay every second of it in slow motion. I've never stopped trying to figure out what I could have done different. I picked up that gun, and the damned thing wasn't even loaded.

It is amazing, how your mind can work in a panic. I scraped Sly off the floor and carried him out to his truck, grateful that no one was around or passing by. I drove him about a mile, to the deepest part of the Tallapoosa River. Then I put him in the driver's seat and sent him to the bottom of that dark water as fast as I could, truck, gun and all. I watched the last bubbles reach up and scream my name; then I ran home and changed my bloody clothes. I took them and Sly's doctored receipts and placed them atop the big red-brown stains on the floor. Then I dragged every hay bale I had to cover the pile. By the time Nancy and Margaret got home, I was still working hard to breathe right. My heart was pounding so hard you could see it through my shirt, and I felt mighty sick to my stomach. I told Nancy, "I'd better go up and lie down for awhile because I'm tired."

Margaret had brought her friend Karen with her, and I heard them outside my window, giggling. I prayed, hoping the Lord was still listening to me, for them not to go near the barn. I tried to think of a reason they should stay away, but I couldn't come up with anything that didn't sound ridiculous.

That night, I let them take my car to a movie in town. I figured it was the perfect time to tell Nancy what I'd done, except I couldn't. The words would not form on my lips. I convinced myself, I guess, that Sly had forced me into violence with that gun. I only defended myself. How was I to know he was waving it around, impotent?

So, I sat there and chewed my chicken-fried steak, concentrating on my next move. It came to me in a rush—I was going to have to burn down my own barn.

When those girls stopped chattering and settled down for the night, I slipped out of bed and left Nancy softly snoring. I didn't even use kerosene; I threw two lit matches, one after the other, onto that tower of hay covering my sins. When I was sure it had caught on real good, I crept back into the house. Five minutes later, I sprang up and yelled, "The barn is on fire!" I ran out there, pretending like I was gonna try to put it out, while she telephoned the fire department and got the girls up.

Watching that blaze eat up my hay, my tools, and my barn was the first of many penances. I know I deserved it, and more. My whole family had tears in our eyes; each of us for very different reasons. Margaret was terrified her cat had been caught in the barn. The Parker boy, driving past, stopped to help and returned Matilda to her safe and sound. I was still limited to one victim.

The next morning a cruiser from the Cleburne County Sheriff's Department pulled into our yard. "You seen Sly MacDonald?" the deputy asked. "His wife Eula says he's been gone almost three days, and that's longer than usual. She's worried about him." I told the officer, "my brother-in-law is known to drink a bit and disappear from time to time. I am sure he'll show up." He pointed to my ruin of a barn, asking when it burned. I told him, "The fire had started in the middle of last night, and I ain't sure of the cause." He asked, "Mind if I poke around the ashes?" "Be my guest," I replied. I even offered him a glass of sweet tea, cool as a November breeze.

The next week passed without much happening; I was trying to figure out how soon I could afford to re-build the barn. Eula called Nancy almost daily, heartbroken on Monday and Tuesday but gradually adjusting to the idea of her no-account husband being gone. She eventually convinced herself he must've run off with another woman; I'm not sure why.

I sinned again, maybe not as deeply, but sinned nevertheless. Judge Parker's boy, Darrell, came to see me that next Sunday. He said, "I'm responsible for the fire, because I tossed a cigarette in the direction of your barn. I will pay to re-build and re-stock it." I sat, frozen, trying to figure out how to respond to this good luck. After all, the Parkers owned half the town; it wouldn't be a burden for them to come up with the money. It gave me a perfectly innocent cause for my fire, still a worry in my mind. I knew Margaret was sweet on Darrell, and he on her. I figured he was probably hoping to get closer to her by spending the next few weeks in my yard. That wasn't necessarily a bad thing. I washed my hands of the barn fire right then and there, with the sweat from my iced tea. I shook Darrell's hand, and let him believe he'd done an awful thing, burning down my nice barn.

I've done penance for that, too. I gave Margaret away at her wedding, looking that fine young man straight in the eye and saying, "Welcome to our family" with a smile. I joined Nancy in the pew and wept tears of shame.

Eula waited two years for Sly to come back, then picked herself up and started seeing Glenn Harrison, a nice sober widower. They ended up having a right good marriage.

Margaret and Darrell had a beautiful daughter of their own, Ellen. They lived in a nice house in town, and Darrell was an attorney with his own firm. He thought of running for state senate, and I hoped no one would ever dig up his accidentally setting a fire in his youth to use against him. I couldn't imagine they would.

My dear Nancy became slower getting around, and the doctors told me my days were numbered. I had a good life, and I hoped all my mistakes would not follow me into the next world.

I tried not to be afraid as I clutched Nancy's tender hand, working to ignore the pain and remembering my better moments.

Growing Up in a Small Town
Lisa—2006

I was never meant to live in the middle of nowhere. I have tried. I kept trying for my husband's sake, because he wanted to live on the land his great-great-great-grandparents lived on, though his family moved away long ago. He wanted to raise our daughter in what he feels is fresh, clean air. He thought she should have her own pony.

I might as well be a different species as far as the locals are concerned. Hunting dogs, gun racks, tobacco juice to spit, recipe exchanges and pot-luck dinners were in vogue. Some landscaped their yards with rusted hulks of cars; some with old tires full of petunias. I did not fit in. I couldn't cook, though Tommy's mom had given me her best Southern recipes. Maybe she was leaving out ingredients to sabotage her Yankee daughter-in-law.

"Lisa," Tommy said, "You have to be friendlier. Most of them are not going to speak first."

I walked into the local food emporium one day, searching for a can of soup among the dusty shelves of Vienna sausages and toilet paper. A few of the men looked at me for three or four seconds, then nodded and smiled. The rest stared at me and got really busy doing something else, fast. The women saw my clothes and heels, then regarded me like Carrie Nation encountering an ornate glass decanter full of whiskey. I made an effort to dress down when I had to go into "town." "Town" is three gas stations and two general stores. One is conveniently stocked with "Fresh Bait." I will not buy bread where worms are sold.

I'm convinced no one ever moved there by choice until they built the lake. It's huge and it's full of large-mouth bass. They actually hold fishing tournaments. Nationally televised fishing tournaments, no kidding. The lake attracted an entirely new crowd, with money and "fancy" trucks. They came here in droves, and spent the day boating and beering. Houses sprung up along the shore, some of which are very well-built and decently attractive—we're talking real brick and glassed-in porches. Unfortunately, they're sharing space with doublewide trailers and sloppy little shacks. I am grateful that we live three miles away from the lake, high on a hill. At least, I have privacy. On the other hand, I hear gunshots nearby during deer season. I am terrified to let Delaney play outside.

When I married Tommy, I thought we'd be living in Atlanta, in civilization with our friends. I thought I'd be shopping and decorating our home. I thought we'd go out five nights a week, like we always had. Somehow, he talked me into bringing Delaney here. Tommy knew my weak moments, and he seized one when she was nineteen months old. There was a bunch of crime near Buckhead that summer, and he convinced me our little family would be safer and much happier out in the country. Tommy is big on heritage and family ties and his newly-discovered ancestral home. His great-great-great-somebody fought for The South in The War, and he's very proud of it.

I grew up Episcopalian. The only churches anywhere near us were Baptist, and that was fine, but Tommy called the minister at the one we visited a "Wejus" Baptist. As in, "Father, we jus' thank you for the opportunity to be here, and we jus' praise you, and we jus' want to say we will try harder to live the lives you want us to live, and we jus' ask that you be with us . . ." It jus' wasn't right for us. Instead, we were driving thirty-eight minutes to take Delaney to Sunday School.

I loved this man since our first date. I knew I would marry him even then, for better or for worse. I would follow him anywhere. I pretty much did that already, because I knew how much it meant to him. I was trying to see the things he saw; I was trying to appreciate the silence, wildflowers and soft green grass.

I was unacceptable on more than one count; first of all, I was born too far north. Second, I was once First Runner Up in the Miss Illinois Pageant, and I might have been a tiny bit vain. I spent a year modeling in Chicago and had a great future ahead there until IBM transferred me. In Atlanta, I was rarely the type of girl needed for the few shoots they did locally. It didn't matter much to me at that point. By that time, I'd met Tommy and had a great job in corporate sales. Then I got pregnant.

I love my daughter more than anything. She is the most beautiful, adorable little girl you have ever seen. She has my nose, mouth and eyes, except hers are brown and mine are blue. My heart had never felt the fierce love that shook me when she was born, and all I wanted to do was hold her and gaze at her face, at the miracle of Delaney. Just thinking about her eyes locked on mine as she nursed made me cry.

She was an amazingly bright and talented four-year-old. She knew her alphabet at two. She could recognize words already. She made little rhymes with me in the car, and I was astounded at what she came up with.

Her ballet teacher said she has real promise, too. She did well in her gymnastics class. My daughter had whatever lessons she needed, even if I had to drive for damn ever to get to them.

I was much happier when in Birmingham. Delaney and I went to her classes; we'd shop, we'd have lunch at Chuck E. Cheese.

Sometimes we drove around and looked at houses. I could see myself living in the older part of Mountain Brook. There are some gorgeous homes there, and one in particular with huge white columns and a balcony in front. If it ever went on the market, I was going to take Tommy to see it. He might consider a move to the city when Delaney was closer to school age, especially if we could live in some sort of antebellum-style Tara-inspired Greek Revival wedding cake topper. I'd wear a hoop skirt if it meant I could enroll Delaney in Deerfield Academy without driving forty minutes each way.

Yesterday as I was driving home from the big-city grocery store, my sweet Delaney, dimpled legs swinging in the rear view mirror, ordered, "Roll down the window, Mommy. I think I gotta spit."

Tommy thought it was hilarious, of course. He would rather Delaney stay home and study Alabama football than learn to pirouette on Saturdays. He promised her they would plant a garden together in the spring, ensuring a house full of red and brown dirt tracks for me, loads of laundry, and ruined little fingernails. She loved riding in his pick-up truck and wandering the woods. He took her fishing, though she mostly just played with the worms, stringing them out across the legs of his jeans while he pretended not to see.

My husband is a good man, and brilliant in many ways. When he got sick of traveling for IBM, he left to start his own software company. Nearly every airline uses Tommy's programs for reservations, flight plans, cost efficiency analyses . . . you name it. Most of the time, he can work from home, with only a few trips to Birmingham each week. Occasionally, he goes to Atlanta or Chicago, but Tommy hates to fly. It's the great irony in his life.

When I fell in love with him, it was partly because of his innate goodness. My husband is a man who believes in absolute integrity, a man of his word. He says it's the way he was raised, and I have no doubt that Tommy Robinson would rather walk on broken glass than break a promise. Certainly, he'd never break a vow.

So why do I feel worried? I used to look up and find Tommy

looking at me all the time, whether I was cooking dinner or brushing my hair or reading a book.

He used to smile and whisper, "Ah, Lisa," as he stroked my hair gently back from my face. All the happiness in the world could be stated in those three syllables. He could look into my eyes forever. He hadn't done that in a long, long time. Worse yet, my husband, who hated to travel, made three trips to Chicago in the past two months.

He's still a very good-looking man, though beer has subtly softened his belly and his hair's thinning a little. You could sort of see it in last year's Christmas card picture, but what's worse, you could notice a change or two in me, too. I didn't think I'd aged much until I saw Delaney's little face contrasted with my own. Almost a perfect miniature of me, only without thirty extra years of sun and stress. Is this what Tommy sees when he looks at me? Is this why I don't catch him looking?

And that is why Delaney went to stay with her Grandma Ellen. Grandma Ellen adores Delaney, the one good thing about her Tommy marrying me. This is a woman who served me boiled okra on my first trip to her home, just to watch me squirm. She was clearly less than pleased about our engagement, though she was impeccably polite from the very beginning. Ellen is nothing if not impeccably polite.

While Delaney baked cookies with Ellen, I went to Birmingham. Everyone thought I was going to see my gynecologist, but I really went to see a plastic surgeon. I wanted to find out about Botox and Restylane and any other modern miracle in his arsenal.

I wanted him to look at me and say he knew a minor thing or two we could do to make the subtle changes I needed. I wanted him to look at me and tell me I was crazy to think I needed anything at all, because I looked far younger than . . . groan . . . thirty-five.

There are few places as uncomfortable as a doctor's waiting room, and Dr. Clarke's was no exception. For the life of me, I can't understand why a plastic surgeon would want an office bathed in fluorescent light. Maybe for the "before" experience. Maybe there was a suite of rooms with rose-tinted bulbs for the "afters."

"Mrs. Robinson? I'm Leslie. Come on back," his nurse smiled, a touch too cheerfully.

How old is she? Has she had Botox? I couldn't help but notice her inflated lips and boobs. Do they get this stuff for free?

I was seated in a very plain, very clinical white room with a couch and an exam chair on wheels. After I thumbed through Redbook twice, the door opened.

"Hello, I'm Dr. Clarke," he said, offering his hand. He sat down and looked over the paperwork I'd filled out. "So," rolling closer, "you're concerned about lines around your eyes," and then he came even closer, his thumb resting in front of my left temple. "Well, we could try a filler, but I don't think you'd see much difference. Botox would be effective, but not really indicated for the tiny wrinkles you have here," he frowned slightly, tapping beside my eye. "You barely have wrinkles at all."

Leslie had followed him in and stood at his side, appraising me. I felt a little smug.

The last thing I expected, the very last thing, was the way he leaned over and pulled my eyelids in various directions. Leslie held up a hand mirror for me, a practiced gesture.

"See how the eyelids are starting to sag slightly, Mrs. Robinson? And look here, under the eye. Those fat pads are becoming noticeable. It's a normal part of the aging process, and very easily addressed." He pushed his chair back. "You may want to consider upper and lower blepharoplasty. It's a relatively simple procedure, performed here in my office. Your recovery would take about two weeks. I think you'd be very pleased with the results." He was staring at me in the most peculiar way.

I was speechless for about thirty seconds, just blankly staring back. I recovered enough to sputter out, "Thank you, Doctor, I will think about it."

"I hope you will, Mrs. Robinson. You are a pretty lady, and you could easily pass for twenty-five after the procedure. You've taken great care of your skin, and it shows. Do you have any questions for me? Leslie will tell you everything you'd need to know about the cost of the surgery, the times we have available, your pre-operative instructions, and so on."

I shook my head no, still stinging. "I don't think I have any questions right now." A smile, a lingering look at my eyes, and he was out the door, carrying a large chunk of my ego.

Leslie offered me brochures on blepharoplasty and Botox. "Okay. The cost of upper and lower eyelid surgery is about $7,600, plus anesthesia. The total would be approximately $9,250, but that would include everything. Dr. Clarke's schedule is pretty open three weeks from now, so we could book your surgery as early as the twenty-first. Do you want me to set up a date for pre-op? That should be at least a week before."

I sat there, mute.

"Mrs. Robinson?"

"Oh, I'm sorry. I need to think this over, Leslie. I'll call you within the next few days."

"Yes, ma'am, that will be fine."

I will never get used to the fact that everyone calls a woman over twenty-one "ma'am" here. I am not that damn old. And Leslie, screw you, you're not that young.

By the time I picked Delaney up—Did Ellen look suspicious? Can you tell if someone's had a pap smear?—I had decided I had to talk to Tommy about this. I could get away with writing a check for minor wrinkle repair, but $9,250 would definitely be a problem. Not to mention the big black eyes. Yes, Tommy would have to be a part of this decision.

How does a good husband respond when his wife mentions she

might want plastic surgery? "No, honey, you look beautiful the way you are." That would win him points, but what if I really wanted it? "Okay, Lisa, if that's what you want, it will be fine with me." Then I'd be convinced he secretly thinks I look old. I don't think Tommy can win here.

Ten minutes away from Ellen's house, with my knuckles white on the steering wheel, I heard Delaney plead, "Mommy, I'm thirsty. Grandma Ellen and I made cookies. With princess sugar on top."

"We'll be home in a few more minutes, Pumpkin. Were the cookies good?"

"Yes, ma'am."

"Did you color? Did you play outside?"

"Yes, ma'am."

"Grandma Ellen is worried about Mama D. She told Granddaddy Mama D has her memory in her lap."

"Memory lapse, maybe?"

"Yes, ma'am."

"Oh, that's nothing, sweetie. We'll go see Mama D next week. She's fine, I'm sure."

Delaney is crazy about Tommy's grandmother, and Mama D is crazy about her.

"We're almost home, Delaney. See the lights? I think Daddy's home already."

Tommy came out to unfasten Delaney and swing her into the air.

"I cooked pizza. A complicated, frozen one."

"Thanks, babe, I wasn't sure what we'd do for dinner. Although Missy Prissy here is probably too full of princess sugar cookies to eat."

Delaney raced around back to her puppy, thirst momentarily forgotten. I started to follow her, but Tommy caught my wrist. "I have something for you. Bought it in Chicago. An early birthday present."

He produced a little blue box, and I opened it to find a necklace;

a gold disc with a "D" in diamonds. Tommy cleared his throat, then took a deep breath. "For Delaney. For the family that we are. For all the things I love about you, and all the things I will ever love about you to come. Thank you for living here, Lisa. Thank you for letting me give this to Delaney. I mean, I know it's not where you want to be." He tilted my chin up to look into my eyes, "But it's just while she's this little. I want her to start her childhood here, and then we'll use the place for weekends now and then. I want us to sit on that porch together when we're old and gray. I want to bring our grandchildren here." He brushed my hair gently back behind my ear. "Ah, Lisa," he sighed, and then smiled and gave me the longest, sweetest, lip-sucking kiss.

Delaney ran by, giggling wildly, puppy bounding at her heels. "Mommy! I saw a lightning bug!"

I think Dr. Clarke can wait. I needed something to open my eyes.

Jillian's Eyes

From the diary of Dr. Rob Clarke—2006

You have to understand how unusual Jillian's eyes are; how differently shaped and colored from the ordinary catalog of human eyes. Hers are deep, deep blue—Lake Tahoe in the summer. They're almond shaped, but far more open than most. They tilt up at the edges. Her lashes are long and black. I look at eyes for a living. I should know.

It's been years since she left me; two-and-a-half years of trying to live again. Waking up next to a woman I don't want to know, muttering excuses and running off to the hospital or the office.

I am a plastic surgeon. I am good at what I do; as much an artist as anyone who ever put a brush to canvas. I have a cosmetics practice, but my heart is also with the Humpty Dumptys in the ER. The ER is where I met Carla Hansen, the mother of a six-year-old boy who'd tipped over a pot of boiling baked beans. Jacob looks good as new after two major grafts and years of healing. Carla looks a little bit like Jillian. She was my first candidate, because her irises are a pretty remarkable dark blue. She was aging—forty or so—and concerned about her lids getting a bit saggy. I told her to come by the office for a complimentary bleph consult. I can't deny that I was excited about Carla, and the opportunity she presented.

Blepharoplasty is not a very complicated procedure. I had lots of time to plan in advance how I'd subtly sculpt Carla's orbital tissue, and stitch a bit differently than usual. For a first attempt, it went very well. Carla has a fairly decent approximation of Jillian's eyes. She's happy, I think, though she has no idea of the artistry I employed on her. She works in my accountant's office. I admit, I was there more than usual after her post-op visits ended. I wanted to see. I wanted Carla to wear a blue dress, but couldn't exactly ask her to.

Eight more pairs of blue eyes; eight more surgeries followed with varying rates of success. It takes a long time to find the right eye color, though no one will ever have Jillian's. I just try to come close. Today, though, I met the best one ever, Lisa Robinson. I told Leslie she'd better follow up on that one. My God, she's perfect.

These women—my selected few—live in my city. It's only natural that I should look for my various homages to Jillian in the grocery store, at the post office, in the gym. All of them have been tremendously improved by my handiwork. These eyes are my little masterpieces.

Jillian Hodges, 1998

When I graduated from Mercer, I knew I had exactly one summer before Mama would insist I come home and help Daddy with his practice. I had already cruelly disappointed them by failing to apply for veterinary school, despite the campaign Mama had been waging since I was old enough to pet a puppy. Dr. Hodges is the best-loved, large animal vet in Fulton County, and everyone there has been waiting for me to add my name to his rusty old shingle since I went away to college.

I had other ideas. Like the Peace Corps. Making a real difference in this world, not helping Mr. Dunfree's mare to foal. I convinced my parents that I could go back to school eventually and apply myself to becoming a vet, but I needed to see how my skills could help in third world countries first, starting in September. A long, lazy summer stretched before me; then I would go forth and do good in the world.

Danita changed everything.

She called, breathless and excited. "Jilly, Greg's taking me to Tahoe! You have to come, Jillian. No excuses, you know how long we've talked about going there. Becky's going, and maybe Dart and Terry, and I think Jenny, too. We're leaving Wednesday."

I wanted to say no. I had plans for June. I longed to relax and cocoon in my childhood bedroom; to look at my 90210 posters and grin lasciviously at Jason Priestly. I needed to plan exactly how I was going to change the world. I yearned to wear short shorts and flirt at the Piggly Wiggly. Drink beer out by the lake, watch the sunsets, see if Steve was in town, and if he ever dumped that tramp Katie.

"Dani, I just got home," I wailed, "Can't we go in August? It will be so hot here in August. We could go cool off then. We could go to Lake Tahoe and Yellowstone and Yosemite and wherever you want, but please, can't we wait a few weeks? I thought this was going to be an August thing."

"No, Jello-Ann. We can't wait. Won't fit Greg's schedule. Besides, you need to get away from Fur Manor as soon as possible, before they talk you into becoming Mistress. Come on, Jilly. You know you want to."

Kinda, but not really. I gave in anyway.

When you land at the Reno airport, all you see is brown hills and flashing casino signs. Brown mountains. They don't look like Georgia mountains. The drive to Lake Tahoe was pretty disappointing at first, especially in the Nissan head-of-a-pin rental Dani had arranged. I was squished up next to Dart, whose real name is D'Artagnan. Mrs. Healey was probably the only lady in Georgia with an Alexandre Dumas fixation. Dart and I haven't been close friends, exactly. He used to find every excuse in the world to brush against my boobs in high school. Very annoying.

Dart had grown up a lot, and seemed to have left his boob-brushing days behind him. Either that, or our back-seat-squishiness was adequate for his needs. We were excited to be this far from home. Lake Tahoe had always been Dani's dream, but at first sight it took our breath away. So beautiful, so blue. You had to wonder what the first settlers thought when they finally reached the top of those mountains, and saw this enormous jewel glittering below them.

Dani turned to regard me in the back seat and informed me, "Jilly? We're staying at a Holiday Inn, but it's not your usual Holiday Inn. It's supposed to be kind of out in the woods. Raccoons peeking in the window. We can walk down to the lake."

She envisioned us water skiing and boating and jet-skiing every day; hitting the casinos by night. My best friend had been planning this since ninth grade, after all. My version was more shopping every day, and hitting the casinos all night. Have I mentioned I'm not much of an outdoorsy girl?

We pretty much fell into a pattern. Sleep till noon. Dani, Greg, Dart and Becky would set out to display their athletic skills; Terry, Jenny and I rushing off to explore shops and restaurants and hike around Heavenly, the ski resort perched above the town. Four o'clock, we would gather back at the Enchanted Holiday Inn Forest. Raccoons would saunter into the room, if you'd let them. There were drinks at a few choice spots, and then twelve hours later, back to bed. Usually singing, arm-in-arm, with Dart occasionally brushing whatever he could, whispering sloppily in my ear.

It was perfect. Except I didn't have a boyfriend. It was never going to be Dart, but not for his lack of trying.

Wednesday afternoon, I was alone for once, sitting on the deck behind our room. I was half-asleep, trying to hold my book up, when I spotted a raccoon racing across the grass, not fifty feet away. Hard on his heels—his little furry paws—was a very cute guy, running and yelling something indecipherable. Curly brown hair. Six feet tall. Running shorts and a t-shirt, legs not too skinny. Probably late twenties. Exasperated.

"Excuse me, sir," I offered, "did that raccoon accost you? I am the daughter of a trained veterinarian, and I'll be happy to assist you."

Where was this coming from? I was usually frozen by attractive men, not chatty. Certainly not first to speak. Vacation woman boldness. I wished I could be Vacation Woman at home.

"What?" he replied. "He stole my watch, the little bastard. I took it off for one minute while I was tying up the boat. I'm hoping he discovers it's not edible," he continued, "though I'm also kinda hoping he chokes on it. Dammit, I lost him. Did you see where he went?"

He turned back around and grinned at me. What an adorable smile.

I was grateful I bothered with mascara and lip gloss earlier. And that I had put on my new white shorts.

I walked over to the edge of the porch and extended my hand. "Jillian Hodges. We're here on vacation. I guess that's obvious. I'm from Georgia. My friends are all out. I was just reading." I babble a lot when I'm nervous. It's very embarrassing.

"Rob Clarke. Nice to meet you, Jillian. Do you know what time it is? I'm due home at 4:30."

"It's 4:15."

"That gives me just enough time. I have to help my kid brother set up his computer. Will you be here much longer, Jillian Hodges?"

"We're leaving Sunday, so I have three days left. My parents are planning to enslave me in an animal hospital."

"Before you succumb to that fate, why don't you meet me for dinner? Will your friends mind? There's a great little Italian place called Romeo's a few blocks from here."

"Um, yes, that would be good. About seven, okay?" I can always get Dani to call my cell and rescue me on cue if necessary.

A dazzling smile. "I'll see you then, Jillian. I'll be the guy with no watch on my wrist." He turned and ran off toward the street with a backward wave. Nice running shoes. Athletic. He'll hate me when he gets to know me.

At 6:45, I set out to walk to Romeo's. Fateful Shakespearean name restaurant. Jillian, beware. Rob was waiting for me by the door, leaning against the wall, with his naked left wrist extended. As if I could forget that grin.

And I couldn't. We walked by the lake and sat under the trees talking until three in the morning. Our kiss goodnight was the sweetest, hungriest, longest kiss I'd ever felt. We were pretty much inseparable the rest of my time there, and he promised he'd meet me in Atlanta in July.

Two years later. I never joined the Peace Corps, or went to veterinary school. Rob and I had a very traditional Southern wedding on Tybee Island, with dozens of my sobbing aunts and smiling uncles and ten of his closest friends and family. We lived in Birmingham while Rob did his residency, and I was happy because I could visit Mama and Daddy pretty often. I taught second grade, and I loved my kids. I told myself 'I'm doing something noble.' The only thing I was absolutely sure of was that I loved my husband with all my heart. For our second anniversary, I bought him a watch we couldn't really afford, engraved simply, "Thank you, raccoon."

Dr. Rob Clarke—2006

On Tuesdays, Jilly dropped me off and picked me up after my shift; usually midnight. It's late for me, but she's a night owl. My schedule was ridiculous then, and fifteen minutes in the car was a nice way to catch up. Several days a week, I was home sleeping while she was teaching. I missed my wife.I kept telling her it wouldn't always be this way; I was going to start my own practice in another six months. I had student loans, we had rent to pay, Jilly had shoes to buy. I met with the bank twice about the financing. We could've made it work. We needed a normal life, with neither of us falling asleep in the middle of a conversation. We wanted to climb into bed together at midnight every night. We were shooting for normal. Soon.

My wife was the best teacher Forrest Elementary ever had. I

know she had all kinds of plans to change the world, but she was doing it here in Birmingham, one kid at a time.

The mom of one of her students was in the ER, with two severed tendons in her right hand. When I checked on her after surgery, she asked if I was Mrs. Clarke-the-teacher's husband; she'd heard I was a doctor at St. Vincent's.

"Yes, I am," I told her. "Do you have a child in Jillian's class?"

"Oh, I sure do, Dr. Clarke. He's actually my grandson, but we're raising him as our own. His mom—well, she can't take care of him right now. And your wife has made all the difference in the world for our Gabriel. Last year, he cried every time he had to go to school. He refused to speak in class. He barely made it into second grade. But Mrs. Clarke has been so wonderful to him. She got him involved in helping the other kids with little chores, and he has friends now. She stayed late three times a week helping him learn to read. She brought him a cake on his birthday, Dr. Clarke. She has made that boy know how special he is, when none of us could after his mama left." She wiped a tear from her cheek. I'm pretty sure it wasn't from pain.

We tried to get out of town on weekends and explore. We went to Cheaha State Park, which Jillian had heard was the highest point in Alabama, and very beautiful. It was a perfect November afternoon, with a gentle sun coating light over everything like golden syrup. Jilly and I climbed out to the edge of a rocky cliff with our picnic, surely far beyond the government-endorsed safety boundary—and definitely, the common-sense boundary. It was worth it for the spectacular view, though. We were hidden from all the tourists on the platform near us. We'd sneaked in a bottle of champagne, and she'd packed some kind of fancy chicken salad sandwiches and chocolate cupcakes. And we sat there, together, the only two people in the world. "Look," my wife said of the landscape, "It's a jeweler's exposition of miniature round sapphire lakes and emerald-cut topaz fields, with red and orange maples and oaks in attendance." When she told me that, I knew she'd describe it to her class exactly that way on Monday. I was married to the world's most beautiful poet. We laughed, we dreamed about our future, we decided that our favorite baby name was Joshua. We couldn't pick a girl name, and Jilly said we might have to settle for Joshuette. Driving home that day, I was convinced that no man had ever been happier than I was at that very moment, with her hand in mine.

I am not a Christmas shopper. I panic and run out at the last minute, and I know I've disappointed Jilly over and over with my clumsy gifts. This year, however, I'd thought of the perfect surprise for her. I designed a deep blue sapphire heart necklace surrounded by tiny diamonds. It's the perfect blue. The blue of Lake Tahoe, of Cheaha's lakes. The blue of Jillian's eyes. I thought I would pick it up tomorrow, while she's working.

Tuesday night was usually slow. We had one fool who sliced his knee with a chainsaw earlier, about four o'clock. He was stone-cold sober, too. A head laceration and a badly cut finger. Danielle, pudgy but cute in her frog-covered scrubs, said she was going to the cafeteria. Danielle leaned toward pediatrics. And weird scrubs.

Just before midnight. Things were pretty quiet, so I went to get a cup of coffee in the lounge. Damn, damn, damn—I got a page. MVA. This was going to make me late. I should have called her.

The paramedics banged through the door, and I gloved up and got ready to see what I could do. We were all running, running. I saw my patient, but it couldn't be my patient, because it's Jilly. The next thing I knew, Dr. Morgan was elbowing me aside, and Tammy started ushering me out of the room. They wouldn't let me back in there, and I tried with all my might to pray, but I couldn't slow my mind down enough for that.

Randy Morgan came out with that look, the same look I've practiced for awhile now. Steady gaze, sympathetic, not overly emotional, matter-of-fact. It says, "I'm going to help you process this news." I didn't want to process this news.

They let me into her room, and I held her hand. I don't know how long I was there, but then her parents were by my side, followed by her friends. They said it's time to leave, but I wouldn't go.

They must have called Alan Klein, the staff shrink, to lead me out. I remember all soothing words and firm support.

What I remember most is people whispering around me. Like I didn't already know the most horrible thing I could know.

I refused my mother's offer of Christmas at Lake Tahoe, which would've been several circles of my own personal hell. I refused all offers for Christmas anywhere. I stayed home. I went to the cemetery and talked to Jillian. I stared at our bedroom ceiling and talked to Jillian.

I drank a lot. I didn't shave. People called, and I answered, but only if I thought they might drive over to check on me.

I'm sure the whole world was whispering about me by January tenth, my first day back at work. The bearded, red-eyed doctor. He lost his wife.

It was around this time that someone told Dr. Klein to check on me. He started turning up in the ER unexpectedly, and even risked hospital food to sit with me in the cafeteria. It was apparent that I should ask for professional help, or the hospital administrator was going to order it. Either way, I was going to end up doing couch time somewhere. So, I sat in Alan's beige office and told him I was fine. I was resuming my life. We met weekly for eight months, until he agreed I was fine. I was ready to open my own practice, and do some cosmetics on the side. Alan thought it was a good idea—a fresh start, a focus other than emergency surgery. I was looking forward to the change, and excited about the challenges.

I will look into my wife's eyes again someday. I know it.

Awakenings

Leslie—2006

I was excited, terrified, and a little queasy, shaking all over.

I was in Room 306 at the Sheraton, wearing a black bustier with garters, sheer black stockings and four inch heels. I was scared to death of what we're about to do.

I arrived early to get dressed and meet him at the door. To adjust the lighting. To choreograph this.

I was about to do the thing I swore I'd never do; the thing I dreamed about. The thing that kept me awake at night; that made me shiver when he's stood close to me. The thing that made it impossible to work beside him without smiling.

It started with simple workplace flirting, nothing too overt. It wasn't going to be anything more than that; a hand on the arm, a brief neck massage. But we spent most of our time together, and somehow, I got to this point. Sitting two feet away from him, pulled like a magnet all day long. I've never felt anything like it, ever.

He knew for a long time that I was falling for him; I'm sure he could see it in my eyes, in the way I dressed for work, the way I did my hair and make-up. The man had to know I was getting up every morning, eager for it to be just the two of us there before everyone else.

And so, he finally asked, "Leslie, want to have a glass of wine after work one night? Just a glass or two of wine, to unwind after a long day?" Then the two of us decided we'd like to get together again sometime.

We met for dinner once, and for drinks twice. It was hard to find time and privacy.

One afternoon, we were finally alone in the break room. He locked the door and kissed me, long and slow. I became weak in the damn knees. I told him, "I want this to be more than a flirtation." I wanted to be with him. In every possible way. I was married, but I wasn't thinking about that.

At six-thirty, I was dying of anxiety. I wished I had brought a bottle of champagne. I wondered if I should order one, but I was already afraid of someone, anyone, seeing me.

I looked in the mirror. The boobs are good. The tan is just right; I've been careful about lines. Waterproof mascara. A bit of lip gloss. Hair blown out this afternoon, soft and long.

When I started working at his office, I replaced a woman named Adele who moved to Missouri. Everyone had gotten used to Adele, and way she did things. They all loved her. They still love her but she never looked like she worked in a plastic surgeon's office. Adele was more the nurturing pediatric nurse type. You'd expect her to hand you a lollipop after your Botox injections. I worked side-by-side with her for two weeks, learning his likes and dislikes; the do's and don'ts. Rob's were pretty simple. The usual pre-interviews and chart placement. Knowing what tools he required, and when. Explaining procedures with, thankfully, the help of brochures. Learning the fee and cost schedule—new to me, but there's no such thing as insurance in that office, only rarely—everything was considered cosmetic. Most of it is common sense. They were there because they were unhappy with something. We fixed it, and made sure they felt really good about the results. He liked his office tidy; he was a clean desk freak. I thought it odd that there were absolutely no family pictures, not one. I found out later what had happened to his wife. It broke my heart.

I wanted to hold him, to comfort him. More than anything, I wanted to be what made him happy.

The clock was crawling. Every time I looked at it, it seemed like the numbers hadn't changed. I tried the radio, which someone left on AM. It came alive with loud crackles of static. I searched FM, but there wasn't a good station.

I should have brought a cd. But what would I have chosen? I didn't know what kind of music he liked. I didn't know his favorite color. I didn't know his favorite movie, his earliest childhood memory, his favorite TV show. I didn't know if he watched TV.

There was a lot that I did know. Our birthdays were one day apart, though he was eight years older. He was from Lake Tahoe, Nevada. He favored jeans and button-down shirts under his white coat. He loved spaghetti and good wine. He was allergic to penicillin. He had a great smile. He ran in the mornings before work. He did a hilarious Bill Cosby impersonation. He loved stupid puns as much as I did, and we read a lot of the same books.

I felt right. For me. For him. It's like I was in his life for a purpose. Fate had brought us together, and there had to be a reason for this attraction between us. The man had been through so much, and seemed ready to start over. With me.

Jerry might have been much happier without me. Somewhere in the past few years, we lost our way. We had grown apart. We fought over stupid things, and he was off with his buddies almost every weekend. I think it was his buddies. Maybe Jerry had been unfaithful to me. At least, we don't have kids.

My heart was pounding now, and all I could do was stare at the door. I popped an Altoid into my mouth and waited. The traffic was heavy. What if the front desk told him the wrong room number? I wondered. Relax, Leslie, relax, I told myself. What if Jerry had found out about this, somehow? What if he was downstairs in the lobby, confronting Rob right now? How in the world could he have known? Jerry was supposed to be fishing in Centre with a bunch of guys from his softball team until tomorrow night.

I laid down and waited. Rob would walk through the door in a minute. I wondered if he'd use his key. I had thought he'd knock, and I'd go to meet him. I arranged myself on the bed and adjusted the bustier.

I picked up the phone to call his cell. It rang and rang, then went to voicemail. I hung up.

I heard footsteps in the hall, and I smiled. Then I heard little kids, and realized it's a family walking by. I called his cell again. Nothing. I jumped when the room phone bleated.

"Leslie, It's me. Will you come and meet me in the hotel bar?"

Okay. That was good. That was fine. We'd relax, unwind, talk. I layered a black cashmere turtleneck and black pants over my Victoria's Secret outfit. The effect was nice. I resisted the urge to wear sunglasses and my scarf, Jackie O-style. We were co-workers having a drink after work on a Friday night.

Rob was in a booth in the back of the room, twirling a martini around in both hands. He was watching it like olives were the most entrancing objects he'd ever seen.

I slide in next to him. "Hi."

"Hi." A quick peck on the cheek. "You look pretty."

"I looked prettier on the bed," I smiled. "Why are we here?"

"Leslie, I wanted to talk to you about some things," staring at the martini again.

"Things? Okay."

"You know about my wife?"

"Yes, Rob. Adele told me about her accident. Four years ago, right?"

"Almost. Leslie, I don't know if we should be here tonight. There are some . . . I haven't . . ."

The waitress appeared. This night is all about great timing. "I'll have a glass of chardonnay, please. House is fine." The waitress nodded and walked away.

"You haven't slept with anyone since your wife?"

He winced slightly. Then he smiled a little and shook his head. "I've slept with plenty of other women since my wife died. That's not it. That's not it at all. The difference here is that I think you're looking for something more, and I can't give it to you. You're married. You're risking a lot here," he glanced toward the empty tables around us. "You are an incredibly attractive woman. You know that. But I am not going to fall in love with you, Leslie. And you are going to end up hating me."

Noble. Damned freaking noble, Rob. "I don't know what to say." I was fighting desperately not to cry, because I felt thoroughly humiliated. I was not going to humiliate myself further by asking why not. That was the thing I wanted to ask. To scream. Instead, I managed to smile. "So, being with me would be a huge mistake. You were confused. We will pretend like nothing ever happened, Rob?" Sure. I will walk into the office Monday, and ignore you. I will hand you scalpels, blade first. I will tell Melanie and Carla you're impotent. I will tell the UPS man too.

"It won't be for too long. I've decided to sell the practice, Leslie. I need to make some changes." He shook his head, staring at the damned glass. "When I lost my wife, I . . . I went a little crazy. I haven't made the best decisions. I haven't done the right things. I'm trying to do that now."

"Why the hell did you wait until tonight, Rob? Why did you let me think there was something between us? What the hell happened between Wednesday and tonight? Between today and tonight? Dammit, Rob, why did you set this whole thing up? Why did you kiss me? Why . . ."

"Because I'm a man, Leslie. Because I'm a dog. The Mad Dog-Man of Birmingham." He rolled his eyes. "And you made it clear you were available. Like I said, I'm trying to do the right thing." He looked at me, then back to the glass. "I knew this was wrong on Wednesday. I knew this was wrong this morning. There was never a right time to talk to you about it. I'm sorry it's now. I'm sorry if I hurt you. I don't have an excuse. I couldn't call you and cancel, though. I thought we should talk in person. I thought I should show up, at least."

The waitress returned with my wine and a new drink for him to stare at. "Would you like to see a menu? We have a selection of appetizers available in the bar." She looked bored. Maybe she should have eavesdropped on our soap opera.

"No, thank you," Rob said, turning to me, "unless you're hungry."

I shake my head no. I will not be hungry for a long time.

"How long have you been thinking about selling the practice, Rob? Don't you think you should have told me?" I was starting to fall apart, bit by bit. I had to be careful not to sound whiny. I had to hang onto my last shred of dignity.

He shifted his weight on the seat, clearly uncomfortable. "Do you remember last Christmas, when I went home to Tahoe?"

I nod.

"My mom is getting older, and I started thinking about it then, I guess. I stopped in to see a friend at Barton Memorial." He paused, looking off into the distance. "I want to do what I set out to do, Leslie, years ago. Reconstructive surgery, like accident or burn victims. Lake Tahoe is a resort town, with skiing, snowboarding, parasailing, hiking, and 24-hour free-flowing alcohol. There's no shortage of trauma. And," he sighed, "Jack Healey wanted to put in a satellite office for BodySculpters downtown. He'd be first in line to buy the practice. I'm done with cosmetics, Leslie. I'm done with eye jobs, implants and Botox. And Jack will hire every one of you. He pays well, very well." Back to staring at the drink. The olive looked like it was staring back, almost. "Do you remember the bleph consult we had a few months ago? Mrs. Robinson?"

I nod.

"She's thirty damn four. She looked fine. I should have told her to slather on the sunscreen and come back in five years. Instead, I sat there selling her an eye job."

"I know. I was there. It's cosmetic surgery, Rob. Elective surgery. You couldn't exactly be expected to dissuade her if she wants to look younger."

He looks off again. "You don't understand, Leslie. Trust me, you don't."

I was trying to process all of this, and my mind couldn't accept it. I wouldn't ask, but despite myself, I still wondered if I could fit into his plans anywhere. What if I were willing to move? To follow him to Lake Tahoe?

"And, well, I saw an old girlfriend when I was home. I talk to her now and then."

"An old girlfriend." Kill me please. I was an idiot, a love-struck teenager in a thirty-year-old body.

I had to get out of there. "I'm leaving now, Rob. Are you going to stay here, or what?"

"No, just leave the key in the room. It's on the corporate credit card." Of course. No one would suspect a thing; we sent post-ops here occasionally. I think we even got a discount rate. It was why I knew the sunglasses and scarf would look normal on the way in.

"Okay." I thought I'd empty the mini-bar, and drink it when I got home. I gulped the rest of my wine and slid out with as much grace as I could muster. "See you Monday. I think. I don't know. Bye, Dr. Clarke."

"I'm truly sorry, Leslie." A heartfelt glance for me, then one for the olive.

The Heart of the Family
Tommy—2006

"Hey, son. Come on in. Say hello to Annie," Dad said, holding the screen door wide for me.

Annie, the world's oldest and fattest Cocker Spaniel, wagged her body. Her tail followed.

"Dad, this dog has no legs," I commented.

"Sure she does. Her body kinda hangs over them," he said, closing the door. "She has paws down there, too. We've seen 'em."

Annie slowly crossed the room to her bed and collapsed with a grunt, a large tan footstool with head and tail. She'd been going deaf for at least two years, though she still heard the can opener and the doorbell, her two important sounds.

"Have a seat. Your mother's in the kitchen, but she'll be in here soon. She's been killing fatted calves ever since you said you'd be coming home for lunch today. At eleven o'clock, I spotted potato salad, macaroni and cheese, fried okra, fried chicken, green beans, and lemon meringue pie." He raised an eyebrow. "She's been back in there since she ran me out," he added, "I'm sure there's more."

Mom's lunches usually induced naps, if not comas. It's like she's expected a crew of field hands.

"Son?" she called from down the hall. "Is that you?"

No, Mom, It's the leader of a starving third world country, here to protest.

"Hey, Honey. Lunch will be ready in a few minutes. I hope you're hungry." She sat next to me on the couch, settling for an awkward couch hug. I saw Dad mentally deduct five points for my not getting up when my mother came into the room.

"I got some fresh tomatoes from Lily. They're really good. Do you want sweet tea or Coke with lunch?" She shifted to the edge of the couch, turning to face me, ankles crossed properly.

"Tea's fine, Mom. How is Lily?"

"She's doing a lot better, but Millard is still having a lot of pain in his hip, and they think they may have to operate. Lily says sometimes he can hardly get out of his chair, but Todd comes over and helps. Did I tell you Lacie Miller is going to have a baby? June is so excited. And Mrs. Cobb is in the hospital. She had her gallbladder taken out—I'm going up to see her tomorrow. Oh, and Garrett Smith is in big trouble."

"What did he do?"

Mom looked at her lap. "They say he stole a car this time. They're fixin' to send that boy to prison. Poor Lena is heartbroken."

"I'll bet."

"How is my beautiful Delaney? Did she go to ballet last week? Lisa said she might be getting a cold, but she hasn't called back about it."

Dad smiled slightly to himself, and deducted ten points for *uncommunicative woman you married.*

We needed to get into the dining room to eat.

"Delaney's fine, Mom. It was probably an allergy. She is at her tumbling class right now, in Birmingham."

"I don't know why y'all insist on living way out there, Tommy. I can't believe the driving you two do, almost every day. Even so, I hardly ever see Delaney."

"I think I'll go wash my hands if lunch is about ready, Mom." I stood, poised to sprint for the hall bathroom before she could think of a reason I should sit back down. After all, we'd be at the table in a few minutes. I needed to save some energy for that.

Dad sprang into action, the cavalry to my side. "Let's see what you've cooked up, Ellie. I'm starved."

Annie lifted her head briefly, and then resumed her nap in the absence of the can opener or doorbell.

Turned out Mom was serving everything Dad had seen, plus biscuits. My mother makes the world's best biscuits—soft, melt-in-your-mouth biscuits, sliced tomatoes, and some leftover ham.

As she placed all of this on the table, my mother said, "I'm not sure I put enough salt in the beans. And the biscuits may not be done enough. Oh, and there's no egg in the potato salad. I'm sorry, y'all, I ran out of eggs."

This litany is as much a part of every meal at Mom's as prayer is in other houses. Of course, the correct response is, "Oh, Mom, these are the best biscuits you've ever made. The potato salad is delicious. So are the beans." Then, and only then, will Mom relax and eat her meal. This has been the routine for as long as I can remember.

"So, have you found a pony for Delaney yet?" Dad asked.

"No, not yet. The only pony Lisa will allow is a half-dead one. She's not crazy about the pony idea."

"Well, I agree with Lisa." Mom agrees with Lisa? Wonder if I can get her on her cell.

Dad looked up, impressed.

"Delaney's very small, Tommy. You're going to have to be careful," Mom said.

"Of course we'll be careful. We'll drug the pony before she climbs on."

"I'm not kidding, Tommy. You saw *Gone With The Wind*. You remember what happened."

"The Yankees stomped us to death with their Shetland ponies?"

"Bonnie Blue Butler," she tossed back. "She had a terrible accident, jumping her pony."

"No jumping, I promise. Mom, what did you want to talk to me about?"

She glanced quickly at Dad, who looked at me. "It's your grandmother. Some of her neighbors are worried about her. They say she sat in the clubhouse for hours a few days ago, and didn't seem to know why she was there. She greeted everyone who came in with a royal wave and a big smile, and then she'd go back to staring out the window."

"Sounds normal to me," I said.

"She was wearing nothing but her nightgown. She doesn't remember it, Tommy. She doesn't even remember walking over there. And yesterday, when we went to check on her, she'd left the stove burner on. No telling how long. It's a miracle she didn't burn the place down."

My grandmother was over ninety, but she had always been very young at heart. Sharp as a tack, and in great shape. It was amazing, how she kept up with Delaney.

"She won't listen to me, Tommy, and she won't listen to your father, either. We want you to talk to her. She thinks you hung the moon, so maybe you can instill some sense into her. It's time we thought about a nursing home." Another quick glance at Dad.

The food lump in my stomach was getting harder and harder. "Mom, I can try, but you know how she feels about that. Can't we consider hiring someone to stay with her?"

"She won't hear of that, either. And I don't know where you'd find someone we could trust, Tommy. People will rob you blind. Old Mrs. Austin had that woman steal her silver, remember?"

"I'll go over there tomorrow, Mom. Lisa and Delaney will be there this afternoon, and that would be the worst timing ever. I'll go.

But can we please change the subject for now? How is your garden doing, Dad?"

The rest of lunch was pleasant enough. "I will not eat again until morning," I vowed to Mom as I pecked her cheek on the way out. I had to fight to stay awake on the drive home. At least, supper for my family rode in the car in six different Cool Whip containers. Lisa wouldn't have to cook, and she'd appreciate that.

Man, how did Mama D. get to this point so quickly? How in the world was I going to convince her of anything, this woman who changed my diapers and taught me to bait a hook and helped put me through college? She's a force of nature, my grandmother. Larger than life.

As soon as I opened the front door, the couch offered to cradle me in its soft embrace. When Lisa and Delaney woke me, it was nearly five o'clock.

"Lunch at your mom's, huh?" Lisa grinned.

"Yep," I said, patting my belly. "Your husband is well on his way to sumo wrestling form." I ruffled Delaney's hair. "Hey, Pumpkin."

"Daddy, Mama D. gave me this." Delaney plopped her arm on the couch. "Look how it sparkles. It's a bracelet. A big-girl bracelet. I can keep it."

"It is very beautiful, Delaney-Doodle. Wash your hands. You have a mysterious sticky substance on them."

"It's not 'sterious', Daddy. It's Tootsie Roll." A giggle and an eye roll, and she was off.

I followed Lisa into the kitchen and swung the refrigerator door open with a flourish. "Look, honey, food. A fridge full of Ellen's Not Very Lean Cuisine."

"Oooh, I see."

"How was Mama D. today? Did she seem all right?"

"Sure, Tommy, she was fine. Why?"

"Because I have been enlisted in a nursing home relocation effort. They think she's getting senile or has Alzheimer's or something.

That she's a danger to herself."

"Oh, no." Lisa looked stricken. "Not your grandmother, Tommy. That would break her heart."

"I know. I know. I'm going over there tomorrow morning. Maybe they're wrong. Maybe she had an off day or two. I'll see for myself."

"Do you want me to go with you? Delaney could stay at your mom's." She wrapped her arms around my waist and looked up at me. "I love your Mama D. I don't want her to have to face leaving her home. And I don't want you to talk to her about it alone."

"This one's all mine. But thank you." I kissed the top of her head.

I didn't sleep much that night, between the afternoon nap and the blender-head. That's what Lisa called it, when you have all these thoughts and worries zipping around in there, keeping you awake. Everything is much worse at three in the morning, and I told myself that things wouldn't seem as bleak at eight o'clock. I was wrong. I kissed Lisa and Delaney bye, and set off to possibly make my grandmother hate me.

She answered the door in her housecoat; not a good sign, since she's always dressed by seven. "Tommy, Darlin', come in! I was just making some coffee. How is my favorite grandson?"

I am her only grandson, her only grandchild. But I would still be her favorite if there were twenty.

"I'm fine, Mama D. How are you doin'?"

"Well, I think I'm fine, Tommy, but you wouldn't be here unannounced before nine in the morning if you thought that was true. Are you worried about me? Did Ellen tell you I paraded around in my nightgown? And it wasn't even my pretty one?"

"Yes, ma'am."

"Tommy," she said, filling our coffee mugs, "I honestly don't know why I did that. And to tell you the truth, I have been forgetting things here and there. But I am not, I repeat not, going to live in a nursing home. That is out of the question. Do you want cream and sugar?"

"No, thank you. They said you left the stove on, too, Mama D. They're afraid you're going to start a fire. I'm worried about that, too."

"Then unplug the stove. I'll microwave my food. Hard to mess that up, unless I throw a bunch of forks in there."

"It's not just the stove," I sighed. "It's any number of things. You are precious to all of us, and we don't want anything to happen to you."

She sat down across from me. "So, you would rather incarcerate me? Banish me to some urine-soaked day room with drooling old codgers? Thomas Edward Robinson, I have lived a long time on this earth and seen a lot of things. I would know if I needed to go to a nursing home. And I don't. Case closed." She got up, preparing to pace. I do the same thing when I'm upset. "Do you want breakfast, Tommy? I can cook some grits, if you watch me closely so I don't set fire to the kitchen. I think I have some donuts in here too." She opened one cabinet after the next. "I'm sorry, I don't have any eggs. That's probably what you'd like."

"I'm not hungry, but thank you. You don't have eggs? Want me to go get you some? I've never seen you go a morning without scrambled eggs, Mama D."

"I haven't had eggs in a month, and I miss them. Dr. Judge thinks my cholesterol is high. No eggs, at least not until my cholesterol is better. Didn't Ellen tell you? She took me for my check-up weeks ago, and Dr. Judge said to tell you hello. And to tell you that your grandmother is healthy as a horse, other than the cholesterol thing. He asked all about you, Lisa and Delaney. He still remembers," she grinned, "when you and Jack played pee-wee football together, and you ran the wrong way with the ball. Twice."

"Hmmm. Nice of him to mention it. Look, Mama D., if you won't consider . . . moving . . . would you think about having someone come to stay here with you?"

"Absolutely not. I may be forgetting a few things, but I'm ninety years old, Tommy. That's bound to happen. And I won't wear my nightgown out any more, I promise." She might be making light of it, but I could see she was worried.

"All right, then." I gulped the rest of my coffee and started for the door. "I'm coming back in two days to check on you. And will you please not cook?"

"I will not cook. Go ahead, unplug the stove. I have plenty of things to microwave, and I don't cook that much anymore anyway. If it means I'll see more of you, by all means, worry about me. Bye, honey." She kissed my cheek. "Give Delaney a big hug from me."

I waved the loose plug at her. "You are officially stove-less. I love you, Mama D."

"Love you, too."

As soon as I got in the car, I called Mom—might as well get it over with. "It didn't go real well. She's very adamant about staying put—alone. I did unplug the stove, though."

"Thank goodness for that."

"I didn't know you took her to old Dr. Judge. She said he pronounced her very healthy."

"Yes, except for her cholesterol. He changed her diet, and put her on some drug. Called it a statin, I think. She's supposed to go back in two months and see if it's helping."

"You'd think that at ninety, you could forget about cholesterol. Personally, I'm going to live on steak, cigars and whiskey after eighty-five."

"You do that, son. As I recall, you tried it in college. I'm glad I won't be here to watch. You'd break your poor mother's heart."

"I'm heading for the office, Mom. I'll call you after I check on her day after tomorrow. If anything happens, let me know. Love you."

"Love you too. Bye."

As soon as I got to my desk, I Googled statins. I couldn't believe my eyes—page after page about possible side effects, especially in the elderly. Dementia. Memory loss. Disorientation. Confusion. I called Dr. Judge at home, and was surprised when he came to the phone. "Hey, Wrong-Way. How are you?"

"Fine, Dr. Judge, thank you. I'm calling about my grandmother. She's suddenly having memory loss, confusion, that sort of thing. Do you think it might be the cholesterol drug?"

"Aw, hell, Tommy, it could well be. Has she had these problems before?"

"Never."

"Her LDL wasn't that bad. Blood pressure was fine. At her age, it's not worth risking side effects. Have her take a pill every other day for the next week, then stop them altogether. I'll need to see her in two weeks, though."

"Thanks, Dr. Judge. Good talking to you."

"You, too, Tommy. Say hello to your family for me."

I called Mom, and she went to talk to Mama D. to adjust her pill reminder box. After a few weeks I plugged her stove back in, though I installed an extra smoke detector in the kitchen. Lisa and I took her to Delaney's ballet recital, and she clapped longer and louder than anyone. We snapped a beautiful picture of her surrounded by twelve little girls in sparkling pink tutus. Mama shined as much as they do. She gave Delaney a "diamond" tiara, which she refused to remove from her head. We took it off for baths, and after she fell asleep.

I visited more often. Sometimes we would eat breakfast; sometimes we just sat and talked. She's decided, "Scrambled eggs have been a part of my life for over ninety years, they will continue to be." It was apparent to all of us that she was doing just fine.

Her only problem was embarrassment over the clubhouse incident, which had been the talk of Arlington Shores, and probably was until the next gossip to come along. I loved her solution. She invited four old lady friends to her condo for a sleepover. They stayed up late and sipped a little wine. They laughed a lot, according to Mama D. In the morning, as agreed, they walked home at ten o'clock in their nightgowns.

We were all grateful that the heart of the family was healthy.

Carhop

Ellen—2006

There is not much about getting older that I liked. I gave up on
'pretty' long ago, and most days was shooting for 'aesthetically
pleasing.' I burned up all summer because at my age it's illegal for
me to bare arms in most states—legs, too. So, it was especially
interesting to contemplate my age when my beautiful
granddaughter reminded me how painful youth could be. She
dredged up all kinds of memories when she discovered my ancient
roller skates packed away in her bedroom closet and asked, "Please,
can I see you skate?"

"Probably, Delaney," I thought, "But it would not be pretty."

I could once sail along like Sonja Henie on asphalt. When I was
sixteen I started working at the Tip Top Drive-In as a carhop. Mr.
Harris had three rules—you had to roller skate a short obstacle
course perfectly, you had to pass his menu test, and you had to fit
into one of his cute uniforms. The Tip Top had a giant neon top hat
as its logo, and each of us girls wore starched white blouses—open
exactly two buttons at the neck, no more, no less—with aqua
cummerbunds and flared black shorts. Our skates were tall white

leather boots; the kind you laced up forever. Our crowning glory was a little black top hat, required at all times. It was held on by a tiny piece of elastic, and encouraged, if not generated, lots of headaches. We didn't care. We were the elite, the chosen few, the girls at the Tip Top. Maybe it was a notch or two or three below varsity cheerleader, but we got good tips.

This was not to say I wasn't plagued by the same painful adolescent self-doubt everyone goes through. My curly brown hair tended to frizz, especially in the summer humidity, when it turned into a living, breathing sponge. I had a pimple that reappeared monthly, a huge red horn on my nose. Worst of all, I had absolutely no boobs. My best friend, Penny Howell, skated alongside me at the Tip Top displaying her 32-C twin beacons of womanhood, hers since eighth grade, oblivious to my torment. I secretly stuffed a little. Padded bras and bikini tops rescued me a bit later in life; until those, I could never even put on a swimsuit and go in the water. My tissues would float away. It actually happened once. I was fourteen, at Panama City Beach.

The few times a year when it got really cold, Tip Top girls were allowed to don long black pants and thin white sweaters, and we had little cotton tuxedo jackets with tails, black kites soaring behind us. From the first day in December to the second week in January, our cummerbunds were bright red and green plaid. Mr. Harris always had red and green floodlights on the white restaurant walls at Christmas time. He also handed out twenty-five or fifty dollar Christmas bonuses to every employee, depending on your length of time in the Tip Top Family. It was incredibly generous at the time.

There were no speakers to bother with at the Tip Top; if you needed anything, you flashed your lights and a carhop would come gliding to assist you. As theatrically as possible, too—the better the skating, the better the tip, usually.

The menu? Far and away the most popular item was the Tip Top burger, a juicy, dripping hamburger unlike anything you'd find in today's fast food places. We ruined plenty of car upholstery, I'm sure, despite the generous paper napkins and cardboard tubs they came with. We served the best ice cream imaginable; Mr. Harris also owned the Tip Top Dairy. I can still taste the banana flavor, so rich, silky and luscious. It had to be 99.9% butterfat.

Working there was absolutely the best thing that had ever happened to me, until Bobby Wayne Tyrell started coming in. Working there and getting to wait on Bobby, well, it couldn't get any better than that—unless he actually asked me out on a date. I had been patiently waiting for Bobby Wayne to notice me since my freshman year in high school. The Tip Top was showcasing me that summer at my carefully coiffed, made-up best, in a really cute outfit. Bonus points for my elegance on skates, too. It was only a matter of time before he was mine, and I'd be cheering for my own personal running back at every one of Lee High School's games next fall. The season before, I'd screamed along with the crowd, "Go Travelers! Go Bobby!" and thought to myself, "Run to me. Who wants more than anything in this world to be wrapped in your arms, looking into your deep blue eyes, threading my fingers through your coal black hair, kissing those soft lips." Yes, my English notebook had "Mrs. Bobby Tyrell" and "Ellen Tyrell" secretly scribbled all over the inside back cover. I was love-sick, obsessed and aching.

And that was not to say that I knew a thing about football. I knew he was a "running back" and his number was thirty-nine. Other than that, I stood with the crowd, sat with the crowd, booed with the crowd, and screamed appropriate phrases along with the seasoned fans. I hadn't the vaguest idea what was going on out there. I was just there for thirty-nine. You're supposed to know and love high school football in Alabama, in preparation for Crimson Tide or Auburn Tiger football; I simply loved him from the bleachers.

Bobby Wayne's daddy owned Chevrolet dealerships in both our town and Gadsden, and Bobby had a cherry red and white '57 Chevy that everyone coveted. I could see him coming from almost a mile away, and the first time he pulled into one of my parking spaces, I nearly died of nervousness before I made it to the car window.

I smiled and recited Mr. Harris' line.

"Welcome to the Tip Top. I'm Ellie. What may we serve you tonight?"

Bobby Wayne, heretofore unaware of my existence, smiled a smile that went straight into my heart and said, "Hi, Ellie. We need four Cokes and four burgers."

I died momentarily and then started skating backwards, flashing my best come-hither look at Bobby and nodding. "Coming right up!"

Bobby's friends found something hilarious to elbow each other about. They were all overgrown football players, and Neanderthalish to me.

I pirouetted a bit on my re-approach, carefully balancing their drinks. I was good. Bobby reached out to grab the aqua plastic tray as I started to position it on the shelf next to him, and somehow, sixty-four ounces of Coke and cubed ice splashed all over him, his white vinyl bench seat, his shiny steering wheel, and his spotless new floorboard. I froze, and his buddies did, too, waiting to gauge Bobby's reaction.

I babbled, "I'm so sorry, I'm so sorry."

He smiled and opened the door, brushing off a river of sticky soda-fountain drink in the process. Then he turned and wrapped his arm around my shoulders, squeezing them and nudging my head under his chin, saying, "It's okay, everyone has accidents." His chest was hard, all muscle. I wanted to stay there forever. I was hoping the other girls saw the full thirty seconds until he released me and looked at me expectantly.

I raced back to the kitchen on air instead of wheels, heart pounding. I brought bunches of napkins and then, replacement drinks. By the time I brought their hamburgers, they were calling me "The Torrent." The Neanderthals were not exactly poets. Mercifully, it didn't stick.

The next week, he came around to show me his car—good as new, cleaned to perfection by the guys at the dealership. "Act like it never happened, Ellie."

After that, Bobby Wayne made a habit of parking in my service section, almost every night I worked. He was always sweet to me, and I started getting ready for work an hour in advance. All I could think of was seeing him, and that smile he saved for me. When Young Love blared over Mr. Harris' outdoor hi-fi system, I told him, "It's my favorite song." I hugged my plastic serving tray across my non-breasts with both arms. He told me, "If you'll take off those skates, I'll dance with you right here." Of course, I couldn't, but oh I wanted to with all my heart.

My mother picked me up every night I worked that summer, sometimes as late as eleven o'clock. She and my dad were the only divorced couple I knew of in my town, and I was embarrassed when she pulled up in her old Buick. Everyone else rode home with their dad or boyfriend. Sometimes Penny's dad would drop me off, if I was lucky. It was years before I could afford my own car. One night, I couldn't get her on the phone to tell her I'd be riding with Mr. Howell. Bobby Wayne was sitting outside eating ice cream, without his Neanderthal escorts, for once. I casually mentioned, "I can't get my mom on the phone," and he told me, "Try again and tell her I'll drive you, if that's all right."

Oh, yes, that was all right.

She answered on the third ring, and said, "That's fine, Ellie." She knew Bobby's family. Everybody knew Bobby's family. It was about ten o'clock, and I glided into the ladies' room to check my hair and dig through my purse for spearmint gum while Wanda covered for me.

The next hour alternated between terror, giddiness and joy. I had to restrain myself from grinning like a monkey with a banana every time I glided past Bobby's car, soon to be the birthplace of my dreams come true. I told every other girl working that night, "My time has finally arrived—Bobby is taking me home." After that, we all stifled grins and stares as we passed his windshield.

At precisely eleven o'clock, Bobby opened the passenger door and I slid across that white vinyl to the center as close as my shyness allowed, waiting for the arm that would encircle me. I could already taste that first kiss. I wondered if we'd do the things my girlfriends and I had discussed at slumber parties, the things I stared at my bedroom ceiling and contemplated. I wondered if my mother would have the decency not to be watching out the front window. We made small talk about school, mine the nervous chatter of a rising junior and his the self-assured advice of a senior. "Mrs. Burgess is who you want for English," he informed me. "Mrs. Tolleson is who you'd better pray you don't get for Chemistry. Football practice is starting in a few weeks. Would you like to come and watch?"

When we pulled up to the curb, I was glad to see no sign of Mom lurking beside the window. The front porch light was on, but I imagined her on the sofa, engrossed in a romance novel of her own. Bobby turned off the car and faced me. "I want to talk to you about something." I nodded, my lips slightly parted.

"Do you think Penny would go out with me?"

I blinked. I rearranged my face with effort. Nine nails were in the center of my heart, and I needed to get inside and pull them out, look at them one by one.

Do you think Penny would go out with me.

"I don't know, Bobby. "You'd have to ask her yourself. Thank you for the ride home." I fumbled for the door handle, where was the damned door handle?

He started the car, and assured me, "I'll give you a lift anytime. Good night!" He waved a little with that smile.

I closed the door as gently as possible. I remember thinking it was very heavy. As I started up the sidewalk to the door, the tears

flowed. They didn't end until two days later. I had become The
Torrent.

Mom jumped up from the sofa, horrified. "What is it, honey?
What did he do to you, Ellie?" She was trying to wipe my face, but I
was sobbing too hysterically for her to make any progress. She led
me to the recliner, sat me down, and knelt in front of me. "Ellie, take
a deep breath. Are you hurt?"

Was I hurt. I was broken beyond any possible repair. I wanted to
die. I managed to catch my breath long enough to tell my mother
the gist of the situation. I didn't want her thinking Bobby had tried
to rape me, or something. Then I resumed sobbing, in her arms now,
one hand stroking the back of my ugly, kinky hair.

"I'm so sorry, honey. I'm so sorry. Ellie, he's an idiot. He doesn't
know what he's missing. You are beautiful, and he's a stupid boy.
He's not worth this. No boy is worth crying over, and the one who is
won't make you cry." She tilted my face up with her finger. I tried to
stop long enough to reassure her, and then I said, "I'm going up to
bed."

She let me stay there until noon the next day; it was Saturday and
Mom had the day off. She was going shopping, and she wanted me
to come along. I was grateful she said, "I understand" when I said,
"I just want to stay home."

Was I going to tell Penny? What would I tell all the girls I'd
informed that Bobby was whisking me off for romance? It was the
first truly hopeless situation I'd ever encountered. In the end, Bobby
saved me from telling Penny by calling and asking her out himself
that afternoon. She, my most beloved friend, turned him down
flatly out of loyalty to me. I never said a word to the rest of them
about it. I assumed Penny did, and told them to keep their mouths
shut.

Gradually, I adjusted to waiting on Bobby Wayne and his friends
again in my new, undesirable persona. I had no idea why he
continued to park in my section, but he did. Other cars with other

boys came around, though none excited me like the one true love of my life did. I dated a couple of them, but have long forgotten their names.

Bobby Wayne graduated and took a little piece of my heart with him off to the University of Alabama, where he flunked out after the first year. He then enlisted in the Army, and went on to fight in Viet Nam. He returned a much older man in his twenties who crawled into a bottle for a few years, then came out and took over his dad's dealership in Gadsden. I lost track of him after that.

Penny and I continued to work at the Tip Top after graduation; I finally bought my own used-but-lovable old Hudson Jet, and she eventually went to Auburn with her savings. I had no idea what ever happened to her.

About the time I got to be way too old for a Tip Top girl, I met and married my husband and settled down to cook and clean house and join the Junior League; Tommy was born two years later. And, I didn't actually meet Tom Robinson for the first time the October day he drove up. He was one of Bobby's Neanderthals, who had always smiled at me from the back seat. I had things all wrong at sixteen. I married a wonderful man.

Delaney wanted me to put the skates on, so I sat on the edge of the front porch and high-stepped across the grass in them. That was not enough to make her smile, so I skated, very tentatively, across the driveway and back. It felt good. It felt right. I knew enough to stop, however, before I fell and broke a leg. Delaney wanted to try, so I managed to put her tiny feet in and held her up, pushing her along on the wheels. She clapped and screamed happily, thinking she was gliding on her own.

Carhop, Part II

Tom

I could not believe the things I did to ride in a Chevy. Admission price to the red and white leather seats was two cold beers each, though Bobby Wayne let us in without them. He was very used to getting what he wanted, Tyrell was, and we did our best for some very good reasons. Girls. Pretty babies. Adventures.

Once, a new Northern girl in school called him Bobby Wayne "Tir-ell". He immediately gave her his trademark smile and corrected, "Tie-RAY-uhl, sugar."

Anyway, if it works out, that gives us eight beers: One for me, one for Moose, two for Hardy, and four for Tyrell. If he has four, though, he will let Moose drive his car. His daddy would kill him for letting anyone else take over the wheel. It's one of many things his daddy would kill him for.

Mr. Tyrell smiled down on everyone in town from his huge billboard on Highway 27. He and Mrs. Tyrell and Bobby were in First Baptist Church every Sunday morning. Tyrell Chevrolet donated a new station wagon to the hospital auxiliary.

Mr. Tyrell pounded on Mrs. Tyrell occasionally, but never where you could see it.

That last thing was not widely known. I knew only because I accidentally dropped in on a huge fight one night, and figured it out on my own. Bobby and I had exactly one conversation about it, and I doubted there would be another. I also knew Mrs. Tyrell started adding vodka to her sweet tea in the afternoons, usually when *Search for Tomorrow* came on.

Mr. Tyrell thought his son was pretty worthless and told him, "You couldn't sell ice water in hell, son." As long as Bobby's not in school or at a practice, he had to be available to come in and perform whatever jobs his father assigned, though. Usually, they were janitorial duties or detailing cars. He was very good at the latter, because every Saturday morning at six-thirty, he was required to drive his demo over to the dealership and do whatever was necessary to make it look like it rolled off the showroom floor. One time, a girl at the Tip Top Drive-In spilled Coke all over the front seat. It took Bobby three hours of scrubbing to remove every speck of that mess. When his father arrived at Tyrell Chevrolet, ten o'clock on Saturdays, his first stop was to inspect Bobby's work. It had better be done right.

He was known to say, "The only reason my father lets me drive that car is that it's damn good advertising." Bobby Wayne had a handsome, All-American look about him. He was a star running back for Lee High School, and he fit the image for the '57 Bel Air Sport Coupe perfectly, according to Mr. Tyrell.

Coach always said, "Y'all are brothers, every one of you, and I expect you to act like it on and off the field." And we pretty much were, and we pretty much did. Except Tyrell was kind of the coolest brother, even cooler than our quarterback, Denny Mason. Being with him was usually a blast. He had a fast car, and he had some sort of radar for fast girls, too. Sometimes there was one, but sometimes they were in groups, if all of us were lucky. If there was just one, Tyrell would take her out to this secret dirt road to the lake.

He bragged, "What starts with a beer in the front seat ends up bare in the back seat."

Usually, though, it was Tyrell and his latest girl in the front seat; me and mine in the back at the local passion pit, the Midway Drive-In. One Saturday night, we pretended to watch *Old Yeller* for the third time. That movie was the best. You knew she was going to end up crying, and you were going to make out. I wished it would have played there for all of senior year.

Sometimes we dragged out near the lake, but not much. Tyrell said his dad could read tires, and racing would get him killed.

We were always at the Tip Top, because Bobby spotted this Penny girl, a sophomore, in school last year. She was stacked, with what he called a classy chassis. He found out she was working at the drive-in, wearing roller skates and a short little outfit. Tyrell had figured out the perfect place to park, where he had the best view of her skating away, his favorite. We ate far too many burgers—his treat, though—while he described what he wanted to do if he skated up behind her. I'm not sure what made him go ape over this particular girl; there were lots of others out there. Moose thought it was because she wanted nothing whatsoever to do with him. I think he may have been right. None of us were going to rattle his cage over it. There was free food, and lots of pretty babies rolling by.

He would have a much better chance with Ellie, the one who usually waited on us. She was cute, and obviously real gone on Bobby Wayne Tyrell. If he asked her out, he would have had it made in the shade. I would have, but she wouldn't even look at me. Moose had an inspiration.

"Why don't you get her friend to talk her into it, Bobby? They're always together, those two."

"Have little Ellie open the door for you," he added with a grin, leering at Penny.

"Tom, what do you think of that?" Tyrell asked me.

I knew exactly what I thought of that. I knew enough about

women to plainly see that Ellie would have never helped Tyrell with that mission, and would have probably slapped him if asked to. But I was not going to be a party pooper; it was apparent the guys thought this was a great idea. Maybe Ellie would have decided she had been getting the royal shaft from Bobby, with his endless flirting. Maybe she would have noticed me in the back seat, trying to get her to look my way.

I said, "Yeah, get her alone sometime and ask her. It can't hurt."

Come Dance with Me in Ireland

Margaret

In my dream, a brown-haired girl ran through a meadow, laughing. She wore a long tan dress; a flower was tucked behind her ear. I sat in the shade of a huge tree and ran my hand along the grass, which was the softest thing you could imagine: lush green velvet. Low stone fences surrounded us, and the day was bright. A cool breeze caressed my face. I was very relaxed, watching her dance and spin.

She twirled, arms outstretched, stopping to pet a fat sheep. Then she walked toward me, smiling, and reached into her pocket. The face looking down at me was much like the one I saw in my own mirror many years ago, around the age of ten. She extended her right hand, tightly closed, offering a gift. It was a diamond, glittering in the brilliant sun that suddenly replaced my quiet shade. She dropped it toward my hand. It fell in slow motion, instead disappearing into the grass. I patted the ground frantically, searching, but I couldn't find it. The girl laughed, and then turned to run to the church that appeared out of nowhere.

I got up and ran, calling, "Stop! Please stop!" It always ended there.

The girl was my great-grandmother, Mary Kathleen Doyle. She worked from the age of twelve as a serving girl for a wealthy English family in town, and grew up to marry Seamus Delaney, an apprentice blacksmith with warm brown eyes and a smile that melted her heart.

The church was an ancient one Carl and I visited in Old Leighlin, County Carlow, Ireland in 1979. Mary Kathleen and her family lived near there until 1849, when the young couple packed their meager belongings and fled to look for a better life in America, in search of food, first and foremost. Mary, Seamus and their seven-year-old son, Patrick, were starving to death along with most of their countrymen. Patrick's baby brother, Kieran, already had, early in the potato famine.

They booked passage on a ship departing Cobh. My grandfather didn't remember much about their voyage other than one, defining thing—Mary got sick and died soon after they sailed. He stood with his father, stoic, and watched as her linen-wrapped body was rolled into the sea; white-hot grief piercing him as she bobbed for a moment, then disappeared forever under the waves. There were three that day, and more joined them in the weeks to come, blessed sweet release from the fever, the hunger, the stench of the quarters below decks. Perhaps Seamus comforted him, but it is more likely that he comforted himself with whiskey if there was any to be had. The little boy who was my grandfather would never again want to smell the salt air. It made his stomach churn, he said.

They landed in New York along with thousands to be processed; filthy Irish—unwanted, unseen, unemployed. They tracked down the Carlow kinsmen who had agreed to shelter them temporarily. My great-grandfather looked for work, walking Hell's Kitchen daily for weeks. He had heard a man with metal-working skills might get on. Young Patrick was set to sweeping and cleaning to help pay for their hosts' hospitality.

Seamus grew more and more discouraged, overwhelmed by bitterness and longing for home. The city was bewildering. The city was cruel. Eventually, he found work in a factory, and developed a plan—they would stay as long as possible with their hosts, paying them rent for the tiny room he and Patrick occupied. Save every single penny they could to move to a better place; possibly to return to Leighlin, though my grandfather said, "We knew we couldn't really go back. Not ever."

He learned quite by accident that his long-gone Cousin Gerald had settled in a place called Alabama. A place where the hills were as green as home, and the rain fell soft. It became an obsession, getting to Alabama. Let the rest of the mad Irish stay and swelter in the factories and serve the rich in their parlors. He and his son would get out "We will be exceptions," he told Patrick, "exceptions among those too beaten to find hope in their hearts."

They traveled by rail to Atlanta, still called Marthasville by some at that point. It was a long, uncomfortable journey, though my grandfather said the accommodations were palatial compared to the aptly named *Perseverance* that brought them from Ireland. Gerald and his fat wife, Bridget, were there at the station with their wagon emptied of cotton, now filled with grain. Gerald was in fine humor, his pockets full of money. My grandfather said, "We picked a perfect time to arrive. It was a beautiful fall day, bright with promise." As he settled in among the sacks, Bridget handed him a piece of peppermint, the first candy he'd ever tasted. He savored it till half-gone, then put it into his pocket for later. Alabama was going to be good, indeed. He fell asleep, dreaming of home.

When he woke, he thought for an instant he'd dreamt the entire past three years. The fields around him, the rolling hills—it looked like County Carlow. He rubbed his eyes; felt the familiar stab of pain where his mother was missing, but it passed quicker this time. He told me, "That day was the one where I came alive again, there in Gerald and Bridget's yard, surrounded by their laughing children as it grew dark. My stomach was full, and my heart was lighter."

The families in the area met occasionally for barn raisings, dances and barbecues. Many of them still spoke with the accents they'd brought from the old countries, Ireland and Scotland. They played the old songs on their fiddles; beat the bodhran drums. Seamus and Patrick knew they had found their home.

With the help of Gerald and several neighbors, Seamus constructed a one-room house for himself and his son. Patrick rose early in the morning to work in Gerald's fields, then walked to school with his American cousins. He made new friends. He helped his father plant his own crops on a small parcel of land purchased from his cousin.

Seamus took his own cotton to Atlanta, a modest crop. He bought a good deal of prime bottomland adjacent to Gerald's, causing a ripple of gossip to spread through the county. The neighbors prattled on.

"Seamus Delaney could never have sold his crop for that sort of price, and you know it, William," Mrs. Delahunty, the town's nosiest housewife, told her husband over breakfast.

Sheriff Green Berry Holder said to his wife, "To be sure, it was a lot of money he paid old Mr. Harris for that land, Katie."

"I heard he stole money in Atlanta," Mr. Evans, the blacksmith, informed the usual group of men gathered in his barn.

Georgia O'Leary, the schoolmistress, remarked, "And where did fine Seamus Delaney get all that money, I ask ye, Mother?"

No one knew. But, legend had it that one Mary Kathleen Delaney of County Carlow, starving and penniless, was released from the employ of the Buxton family after being accused of theft. Theft, specifically, of a jewel belonging to young Eliza Buxton, her mistress. The jewel was never found, and the authorities did not pursue justice.

My grandfather said he never knew the truth. What he did know was that his father thrived in Alabama, branching out after his crops continued to do well. He eventually opened a general store and stable, breeding and selling horses. The little house grew. Seamus helped his neighbors whenever he could, and came to be known as a man of integrity to be consulted on business and personal matters alike. He married Dierdre Reilly in 1853. She was a good and kind stepmother to Patrick.

My grandfather fought in The American Civil War, The War Between the States, in an Irish regiment—the Alabama 15th. He came home to find his family largely spared the devastation so many others had experienced. Dierdre's niece, Margaret Reilly from Macon, was living with his father and stepmother. Her family had not been so fortunate.

She was the prettiest thing he'd ever seen. She scared him to death. Margaret was sixteen that first year, and spent a good bit of time crying when she thought no one was looking. She was in the barn one day, doing just that, when Patrick stumbled upon her. He backed away, but she came over and wrapped her skinny arms around him, sobbing into his shirt. "My life is over. My parents are gone. My brother is gone. I'm grateful to be living here, but it's not home, Patrick."

He told her, "I understand your grief, Margaret. I lost my own dear mother at sea, and the pain took long to ease. Your heart will heal with time, girl," he promised. He stroked her long hair back out of her face, then shocked them both by kissing her. He turned and ran, embarrassed to the core.

They avoided eye contact for a few days as they passed each other around the house. But soon, he found himself helping clean up the store when she was working at the counter. She brought him lunch when he was tending the horses. Sometimes they walked to the lake together in the cool of the evening. She helped Dierdre darn his socks, and delivered them with a shy smile.

A thousand shy smiles later, he asked her, "Will you accompany me to the dance honoring Kerry and Elizabeth?" They were a local couple planning to marry. Papa always had a twinkle in his eye about this.

"Your grandmother, bless her sweet heart, was the clumsiest dancer ever born. Stepped on the feet of every poor lad there that night. I had to ask her to marry me, to save her honor."

I was named after my grandmother, Margaret Ellen Reilly Delaney, and gave her middle name to my own daughter.

In my very old age, I wished I could have talked to Mary Kathleen. I wished I could have told her about the lives her beautiful family has led; of the wonders in this country she could never have imagined. Mostly, I wished I could have thanked her for doing what she had to do to bring us to a better place. I would tell her we completed her journey, and she danced on in my heart.

Outlaws & In-Laws

Ellen

"Ellen," my mom said, "you cannot leave the house wearing that."

"But Mom, it's what Tom said to wear—old dungarees and a warm shirt. I know you don't like it, but it's part of some plan he has. I am not changing, so try not to look at me."

My mother was a master eye-roller, and demonstrated as she walked by. She couldn't stand to see her daughter in pants, much less old blue jeans. I was offending femininity.

When he knocked at the door, she would not let me answer it. I was to remain out of sight until she greeted him and summoned me. Stupid rule designed to make me more alluring. I could have told her a few things about just how alluring Tom Robinson found me, but it was probably best not to.

"Ellie, you look beautiful," he said. I couldn't resist the urge to smirk at Mom, hoping she noted that girls can wear what they want these days and still keep a man interested. Sometimes it was like she froze in the 1930's, staid and uptight as she ever was. I wonder if she even kissed my father before they were married. Probably not. Too messy.

When we were finally in his dad's pick-up truck, I couldn't take the curiosity anymore, so I asked Tom for the tenth time where we were going.

"Out to my old house in the country, Ellie. We still keep the place up, even though we're fancy city folks now like y'all. I want to show you something."

Wherever it was, it was a long drive. We followed a well-worn red dirt path and parked next to a white house that looked like it was all front porch. There were huge oaks in the yard, and a pasture next door. I smiled when I saw them: four beautiful horses, and one tiny colt. They were rapidly approaching the fence. Tom handed me five sugar cubes after he swept me down from the passenger side, stagecoach-style. He had obviously put a lot of thought into that afternoon, and I was more curious than ever.

"Meet Bonnie," he said, gesturing to the chestnut mare, "and Clyde," her colt, who shyly peeked out from his mother's hind legs. "The big palomino is Jesse James; the black one is Doc Holliday and the small white horse with the gray mane is Wild Bill."

"Is your father obsessed with outlaws?"

"No, he says they have the names they deserve. Sometimes they're a little stubborn, but it's mostly his sense of humor."

"They take his oats and hay . . ." I grinned, looking up at him.

"And never let him catch them unless it suits them," he finished. "You and I are going to bribe old Jesse here with some sugar. He's a sucker for it. When he thinks he's robbed us and gotten away with it, I'll put this bridle on him."

Jesse proved a lot more cooperative than his name suggested, and I suspected Mr. Robinson treated every one of these horses like babies. Tom led him through the gate and made a step with his hands, nodding to me to climb on.

"I can't do this, Tom. I've never been on a horse." I got the giggles; it never failed when I was nervous. Didn't matter if it was trying to pass the driver's license exam or meeting strangers at a party.

"I'll be right behind you, Ellie. In front of you, actually, so you can hold on. Jesse won't hurt you."

Jesse swung his head around, considering me with one enormous brown eye. I put my foot and my unbroken bones into Tom's hands, hoping for the best. It took a big swing of my leg, but I made it on. Tom jumped up in front of me, telling me, "Hold on tight."

I decided immediately that this was nice. I could cuddle up close to Tom, who rode like he had been doing it forever. I settled into a gentle side to side rhythm with the horse, who seemed to know where we were going and wanted to take his time getting there. We were loping along next to the highway; there wasn't a car in sight. I rested my head against Tom's back, smiling.

"Hang on, Ellie." The next thing I knew, we turned onto a dirt road and Jesse was running, faster than I thought possible. I was hanging on for my life. We were flying; the old road's oak canopy was a blur when I peeked up. It was smooth, though, and it felt wonderful.

Tom yelled, "Are you all right, Ellie?" I told him I was perfect, and "never slow down."

He laughed and gave Jesse the tiniest kick, urging him on.

I loved this horse. And this beautiful, crisp sunny day. I had never been this happy, and I realized, in a rush, that I was in love with Tom Robinson. I nuzzled his flannel shirt, inhaling Tide detergent and horse aroma in one deep breath.

The horse seemed to anticipate every curve in the road, and I wondered how many girls Tom brought here. He drew on the reins as the road shrank to a grassy path into the woods. At first, it was a very uncomfortable choppy trot but then we were walking again, swaying along past the mossy trees. The sunlight dappled the ground like spilled white paint; there were red toadstools and tan mushrooms everywhere.

I couldn't believe what I saw when I glanced over Tom's shoulder—a soft blue blanket spread next to the riverbank ahead, with a huge picnic basket sitting off to the side.

Tom pulled Jesse to a stop and tied him to a tree. He reached up, smiling, and swung me down in one smooth motion. Then he took my hand and led me to the blanket, waving his arm to indicate I should sit. He was grinning from ear to ear, obviously pleased with himself. He plopped down next to me.

"Isn't the river pretty, Ellie?"

"Yes, Tom. It's very pretty." And it was; the sun glistened on the water cascading over rocks in the middle. It was very narrow at that point, and you could hear the water rushing to its wider, open spaces downstream.

"I have been coming here since I was a little boy. It's a very special place to me."

I couldn't help it. "So, how many girls have you brought here to share it with?"

Tom looked wounded. "No one, Ellie. No one but you."

I needed to learn to keep my mouth shut sometimes, and decided to focus on pulling up weeds and peeling the long stems into thin strips. Tom Robinson was generally a man of few words, and I knew there was a silent gazing at the river coming next. I had to restrain myself from chattering to fill the quiet, something he seemed to crave. After a few minutes that felt like hours, he reached over to unpack the basket, placing a sealed Tupperware cup of sweet tea, a peanut butter sandwich and a box of Cracker Jacks in front of me. I smiled at the menu, but didn't dare hurt his feelings.

About halfway through his sandwich, Tom asked me, "What do you think?"

"What do I think about what?"

He made a face, and it was pretty clear that he meant us.

"Here's what I think, Tom. I think you are the sweetest boy I've ever known. I think this is a perfect day. I think Jesse doesn't deserve his name. And I think you make a really good peanut butter sandwich."

He smiled and relaxed a little, leaning back on his elbows. "What do you think about our future together, Ellie?"

"You know I care about you. We've been together for six months, and I have loved every minute with you." I put my sandwich down and arranged myself to face him. "I love you, Tom." There, I said it. This was silly, I thought. We were almost twenty years old. Did we really have to proclaim that we're going steady?

Tom reached over to kiss me, a slight brush of his lips. This was a very different Tom from the one in the front seat at the drive-in. I was a bit puzzled, since we were alone in the woods with no one but Jesse to see us.

He stroked my hair back from my face, and whispered, "Eat your dessert. We have to get going soon if you're going to get to work on time."

I was confused. I reached for the Cracker Jack box and ripped it open. I do love Cracker Jacks, and I shared the peanuts with Tom because they're his favorite part. The prize, carefully sealed in an original wrapper, was at the bottom—a sparkling diamond ring, a square-cut set in platinum with scrolly engravings framing the stone. It looked old, and very expensive.

I shrieked and turned to Tom as he started his speech, taking my hand in his:

"Ellen Parker, I have loved you for a long time. From the moment I saw you skating toward Bobby's car at the Tip Top, probably. Definitely when you spilled Coke all over us. You were the most beautiful, adorable girl I'd ever seen. So I guess I've been waiting a long time for this." He paused for a deep breath. "The ring was my grandmother's. If you'll have it . . . if you'll have me . . . I want to marry you, Ellie."

For once, I was stunned into silence. I was crying as he slipped the ring onto my left hand. It fit perfectly, just like Tom fit me. It was brilliant and dazzling, and seemed to hold our future together in every color of the rainbow. The river danced over the smooth stones, the sky was the most vivid blue.

In that sweet moment in the sun I kissed him and said, "Yes."

Immovable Objects

Tom

When I was sure I had everything I needed in the old pickup, I turned the ignition key, hoping it would crank. She sputtered a bit, the old Chevy, but she came to life. I patted the dashboard.

"You're a good old girl."

It was Ellie's day to get her hair done, and it was a permanent, so she wouldn't be home until at least three o'clock. Plenty of time. I didn't tell my wife about most of these trips. Too many warnings about the bad part of town. Too many cautionary tales about dope dealers shooting each other. Too many reminders of things that needed fixing here at home. I figured a man ought to have some secrets.

It was going to take at least twenty minutes to get across town, so I opened up my Coke and took a swig at the stoplight. It was my

routine. My ritual. I'd finish half of it before I pulled up in front of
the house; the rest sat in the truck and got warm and flat before I
climbed back in.

I knew Lily Taylor longer than anyone else on this earth, other
than my sisters. When she was a little girl, her mother Beatrice
worked in our house, cleaning and watching us kids.

Lily was usually with her mama, and my sisters treated her like a
dress-up doll when they got her to hold still. Lily was exactly my
age, though, and she and I spent most of our days together, catching
tadpoles and eating popsicles. We would always break them apart
and trade, so she could have a grape half and I could have an
orange half.

Lily was colored in the forties and fifties. In the sixties she
became black. Then in the eighties she was African American. I
always thought colored was the perfect word for Lily; her skin was
a warm, deep brown. When we were little, Beatrice would
sometimes let Lily come to town with my mother and me. I didn't
notice back then that Lily was never thirsty when I stopped at the
water fountain in Rose's. When we got old enough for school, I
missed her a lot. My mother never did adequately explain to me
why Lily couldn't attend Stewart Elementary. It made me mad for
awhile, but I got used to seeing Lily only on weekends. She was a
tomboy, much more inclined toward climbing trees and throwing a
ball than my prissy sisters.

As time went on, we grew apart. It had been years since I'd seen
Lily when I went to the march in Selma with Dr. King. She was
sitting on the bus our group had chartered, talking to a boy with a
huge hairdo. First afro I'd ever seen. I wasn't as involved in the
movement as Lily was, but we lived through that mess together,
whether I was by her side or not. Bull Connor and his fire hoses.
Those little girls getting blown up in church.

Lily went on to become a schoolteacher, the first black teacher
Stewart ever had. It couldn't have been easy for her those first few
years, but when she talked about it, all she mentioned was her

children and how this one had gone on to work at the Redstone Arsenal or that one was in Washington or writing for newspapers. She seemed to remember a lot of names, though she taught for almost thirty-five years. That was a lot of children. I knew she heard from certain ones from time to time, letters and phone calls.

Lily concealed the world's biggest heart in the body of the world's tiniest drill sergeant. She was a small, slight woman with long, straight black hair she got done as often as Ellie did. It was her special vanity. She was not the type of person to run around smiling, but she had a sense of humor that was drier than a drought-plagued creek bed. Lily worried a lot about what the world had come to—drugs, terrorists, children without parents. If you talked about these things and made a point that suited her, the invariable response would be a serious nod and a very deliberate "thank you." Lily went around thanking people for making sense everywhere, handing out her "thank you's" as though she were addressing the good word flowing from her minister's pulpit on Sunday morning.

She told me recently, "I think I'd like to have my own colored water fountain back, because there are way too many white people running around with diseases." We both knew she didn't mean it, because we fought together to share cool water in public.

When she married Millard, he was working at the Housing Authority. I was director there for almost thirty years, and Millard was my right-hand man. We had seen a lot together. We could have written a book, and always said we would someday. He retired two years before I did; he has a bad hip that kept him from moving around much.

Lily and Millard had a grown son named Todd, and he'd made himself a real success in the insurance business. He had two offices, one run by his wife. Their other son, Daniel, was born when Lily was almost forty-two. Daniel is what would've been called retarded when I was a kid; in the eighties he became "developmentally disabled." He was pretty much going to be twelve forever. Lily doted on him; he was her baby. He was friendly and kind—but Lily was always afraid for him to be out in the world for long, without her watchful eye.

The house came into view, a small white wood bungalow with green concrete steps leading to a matching covered porch. I noted that the paint still looked good; I thought Millard must have fixed it recently. There was a swing where Lily sat late in the day, when the heat let up. The yard was a lush and flowered postage stamp.

On Fridays, Ellie's hair day, I was usually there for at least an hour or two. Millard could hardly get out of his chair, and there was always a leaking faucet or a screen door falling off; something I could fix somewhere. Once again, I offered to Lily, "Mother and Daddy's old house on Highway 38 is always available for y'all to live in." She gazed at me across her cup of coffee and turned me down.

"I appreciate it, I do. But no."

She was stubborn as a mule, that woman. Pig-headed. She saw the dope dealers on the corner. She knew that a six-year-old boy was shot near her home, caught in the middle of some damned idiot gang war.

Lily surprised me a few minutes later.

I thought it was because she was worried about Daniel; he couldn't even walk to the store two blocks away anymore. Maybe it's because we had whispered in the kitchen about the wheelchair ramps I could build for the house, because we knew Millard's going to need them. Maybe it's because they would be ten minutes closer to Todd and his family. Whatever it was, I was not asking. I knew when to keep my mouth shut.

"We're paying you rent, Tom. You know I'm not going to have it any other way." She scratched at the tabletop with her fingertip, examining the blond wood. "And we'll have to sell this place first."

"Lily, it's going to take awhile to sell your house. It's not the best time to be doing that, you know." I could see her looking at her stove, remembering all the meals she'd cooked there. Sweeping her eyes up to the window over the sink, where she watched Todd and Daniel play outside. "It's the smart thing to do. You know that. You can have a nice garden out back, and Daniel will have a big fenced yard with lots of room to roam around. No stairs for Millard to climb; I'll have it set up before you move in. Let us do this for you. You know Ellie and I love y'all, and we don't want to have to worry about you every day and night. The place is sitting there. You'd be doing us a favor, keeping the critters from setting up shop. Keeping an eye on everything. Hell, Lily, we ought to be paying y'all to live there."

She smiled, not buying it for a minute. I knew she would let it pass. We would have to argue over the rent thing later.

"Tommy and I will bring both trucks over three weeks from Saturday, Lily. It'll take a few trips, but we can get it done by Sunday night." I reached for my toolbox. "Now, which window is stuck?"

"The one in Daniel's room. Watch out for the Legos."

Millard and Daniel appeared in the doorway, Millard leaning heavily on his son. Daniel had been helping him walk laps around the house outside, something Millard's doctor wanted him to try along with some new medicine.

"Hey, Tom." Daniel grinned at me. "Come look at my football stay-dem. Stay-dee-um."

Daniel had every Lego set ever made. This was his newest creation.

"In a minute, Daniel. Millard, do you have any WD-40?" I had a new can in my toolbox, but I tried to keep Millard involved. I knew it was killing him, me over there working on things he could once fix with one hand tied behind his back. Still could have, if he was able to stand up long enough.

"Sure, Old Man. Lily, look in the cabinet by the back door."

Millard's smile shifted into a grimace as he lowered himself into a chair, hand braced against the wall. "You gonna fix Daniel's window? Thanks, Tom."

Lily turned to hand Daniel the can; it was his job to hold whatever tools I needed when I was fixing things. She found him with his head stuck in the freezer.

"Daniel, I told you, Honey, no more ice cream. We'll have ice cream on Sunday."

Lily worried about Daniel's weight. The only exercise he was getting was helping his dad hobble around, and that was not much.

"C'mon, buddy. Let's see this football stadium."

Lily shot me a look as we left that said, "Don't mention any of this moving stuff to Millard."

I wouldn't. That was her battle, not mine, but she and I both knew who would win.

The window didn't take long, and I was off to figure out why one side of the kitchen sink wouldn't drain. I put a towel rack back up in their bathroom. Lily couldn't think of any more jobs for me after that, so I told Daniel and Millard goodbye and promised Daniel, "I'll bring Annie next time." Daniel loved our dog, and she loved to ride in the truck. The only problem was, I had to lift her in and out of the cab, then install her in the bed if Daniel wanted to ride with her. Annie's older than the Chevy. Wider, too.

Lily walked me to the truck as usual.

"Tom Robinson, you are a good man."

"Don't you forget it either, Lily, especially the next time you're making peach pies. I'll see y'all in two weeks. Delaney is coming to stay with us for a few days next Wednesday, and Ellie has all sorts of plans that include Granddaddy. I think we're going to Six Flags." I closed the door and rolled down the window. "Call me, though, if you need me."

"Bye, Tom." She patted the old truck's door twice and headed back inside, stopping to pull some weeds out of her petunia bed.

When I heard Ellie's car in the driveway, I shoved the rest of the chocolate cake into my mouth and chewed like there was no tomorrow, quickly gulping the last of my milk. I got the glass washed and in the drainer as I heard the door open. It's four o'clock, she'd be starting supper soon, and I didn't need a lecture about fat, sugar and cholesterol, or about ruining my appetite. I figured a man ought to have some secrets.

"Your hair looks pretty, Honey." I kissed her hello.

She wrapped her arms around me and smiled dreamily up into my eyes, whispering softly, "You have crumbs all over your shirt, darlin'."

I took my usual place at the counter, where I watched her cook until she ordered, "Go on and watch TV or something." I loved to watch Ellie cook. Truth was, I loved to watch Ellie do anything.

"You're not going to believe this. Lily finally agreed to move out to the house today. She hasn't told Millard yet, but he'll go along with it."

"Really? That's amazing. Tom, she has to know it's best for Daniel. For all of them. Did she call you?"

I plucked a smidgen of chocolate from my shirt.

"No. I went there to fix a couple of things around the house."

"Oh, Tom, I wish you wouldn't do that. You know they had that gang shooting. It's not safe. Why in the world you insist on going over there and putting yourself in danger is beyond me. You heard about that big drug bust, didn't you? And someone tried to hijack a car at gunpoint, right there on Sixth. In broad daylight."

"Ellie . . ."

". . . and Lord knows there are some things I could use fixed around here, Tom. I can't paint the front door myself, and you promised you'd do it. That was three weeks ago. The paint's sitting out there in the garage. Delaney's coming next week, and you still haven't hung the curtain rods in her room. I can't get the junk drawer open in the kitchen. You said you'd take Annie to the vet for her check-up, Tom, a month ago. And the tub faucet is still dripping . . ."

I jumped in as she drew a breath. "Ellie, Ellie, come on. Give me credit for having a little sense. I'll get to the door, I promise. I'll hang the curtain rods. It'll get done."

"If you say so."

This is what I meant about secrets. One word to Ellie about a trip to Lily's, and I had a verbal barrage of do this and do that.

The nice thing about Ellie's anger was that it passed like a July thunderstorm. In the meantime, avoid metal objects, and try to remain grounded. Sure enough, by the time supper was on the table she was speaking to me again. By dessert, she was being sweet, although I knew I had better act like Jell-o with Cool Whip was my favorite treat in the universe.

The next morning, Daniel rang the doorbell at seven-thirty. Daniel, alone. How in the world did he get here?

"Come on in, Daniel. Does your mother know you're here?" I already knew she didn't.

"No. I want to talk to you. I rode the bus. I don't want to live here, Tom. I don't want to leave my house. I don't want to leave my Legos. I don't want to move."

Ellie came down the stairs, tying her robe. "Hi, Daniel. Would you like some coffee? Some juice?"

"No, thank you." Daniel was staring expectantly, waiting for me to resolve his problem immediately so he could go home.

The phone rang, and I could hear Ellie in the kitchen telling Lily, "Daniel is safe and sound. He's talking to Tom."

Annie waddled in, and I could have kissed her on the lips. "Daniel, why don't you take Annie to the backyard for me? She hasn't been out this morning."

As soon as they were gone, I motioned for Ellie to hand me the phone.

"Tom? I'm sorry. I think Daniel heard me talking to Millard, and somehow decided you're making us move. I am so sorry. If you'll please drive him home, I'll talk to him."

I saw Daniel through the window, following as Annie plodded along.

"I have an idea. Will you kill me if I take him by the animal shelter on the way home? I'm thinking we can pick out a puppy, and Daniel can know it will be his when you get into the new house. You'll have plenty of room, Lily, and the yard is fenced. You know how much he's always wanted a dog."

Lily groaned. She was not a dog person, and definitely not a house-training person. I was counting on the teacher in Lily seeing the incentive value.

After a long pause, she surrendered. "Okay, Tom, if you insist. Think tiny. *Tiny dog*."

The first dog Daniel saw, however, was the one he fell in love with. "What is his name?" he asks the shelter lady.

"We don't know," she replied. "His owners abandoned him. He's fully house-trained, though, and he's very healthy."

The dog was medium-sized, a cross between a black Lab and a . . . Pekingese, maybe. Honestly, he was downright weird looking. A Labinese. He was licking Daniel's face through the cage. There was no turning around at this point. Daniel opened the cage, and the dog wagged his tail like mad, licking his hand.

"Is he gentle?" I asked.

She smiled. "Oh, very. He's really laid-back. Smart, too. He's been neutered, and had his shots. You could take him home today, if you'd like."

"Actually, I need to arrange to pick him up in three weeks. I'll be happy to pay whatever fees you need today, plus boarding costs."

She nodded. "That's not a problem."

Before we left, she took a Polaroid picture of Daniel with his new dog. They were both grinning, I swear.

Lily was waiting out front when we drove up. Daniel was going to get a lecture about running off later, but for now, she hugged him. Daniel handed her the picture.

"He's certainly . . . bigger . . . than I expected." She glanced up at me with a sarcastic squint. "What is his name, Daniel?"

"I don't know, Mama. Tom says I should wait and watch him to see what he's like." That was true. At the moment, all I could suggest was Mophead or Ugleeeeee.

When Lily looked back down at the picture, I noticed a glob of chocolate ice cream on Daniel's arm, and quickly swiped it off. I figure a man ought to be able to have some secrets.

The Parkers, 1974

Carolyn Tharpe Parker

"Hurry up, Darrell. I have to get there early to put these out."

I straightened the pile of flyers with both hands, then placed them in the white box that went on the bench next to the church's front doors. If everyone picked one, we would need more copies. Reverend Gleason wanted the pews packed for the revival.

"Are you wearing your new outfit?"

"Yes, but the damn tie won't tie right. It's too fat. And this looks stupid, Carolyn. I'm too old to wear it."

"Don't say damn. It's Sunday night. You're going to church, and you can avoid swearing for a few hours, Darrell." He looked good in green, though this style took a little getting used to. "It's the new fashion. It's practically the only thing they have at Rich's right now. It's in all the magazines. And it's perfect for the evening service. Did you turn off the television?"

"Yes. And I'm missing *60 Minutes*. Again. Dan Rather was talking about the hippies. I look like a damn hippie in this suit. Sock it to me."

"Don't swear, Darrell. And it's a leisure suit, for when you don't need to be so dressed up. It looks good on you."

"I look like a . . . dadgum . . . hippie, Carolyn. I'll wear it tonight, but after that, you shouldn't expect to see it very often."

"I'll be in the car, Darrell."

"I'll be out in a minute. I have to use the bathroom."

Of course he did. We didn't ever go anywhere anymore without a last-minute bathroom visit for my husband.

Despite my best efforts, the Roberts clan was already there when we drove up. Their children—all ten of them—were running around, throwing parking lot gravel at each other. Darrell shot them a stern look and glanced at our Cadillac. I thought they got the message, though Horace looked like he was waiting for us to go inside. Horace was a sweet faced boy, but he found trouble and if he didn't, trouble inevitably found him.

"Hello, Grace. Hello, Andrew. How are y'all tonight?"

The Roberts family consisted of Grace, Andrew, Cora, Deanna and the rest were part of an ever-changing array of foster children. I don't think Andrew had a job. The state sent them a good bit of support money, and people speculated that about twenty percent of it actually got spent on the children they took in.

"We're just fine, Carolyn," Andrew responded cheerfully. He bent down to pick up a little girl. I was not sure if I had seen her before. "Are y'all opening up? It's hotter than blazes out here."

We formed a parade toward the front door. Darrell helped Grace Roberts flank the end, herding the kids.

"Save me a seat, Honey. I'm going to the men's room."

"Already?"

"The pork chops are settling a little funny. I'll be out in a few minutes."

Reverend Gleason was standing in front of the congregation by the time Darrell slid in beside me.

"Are you all right?" I asked in a whisper.

He nodded, hands folded over his stomach. By the time we sang the second verse of Standing On The Promises I could tell Darrell was really sick. He looked pale; I needed to get him some Pepto Bismol. I wondered if we could slip out somehow. We were right on the aisle. Fifteen more minutes, if Reverend Gleason was merciful, and no one had any announcements.

By the time we walked out Darrell looked a little better, but I told my husband, "We need to get you home to bed." He may have had some kind of stomach flu. I hoped not, but on the other hand, I knew I didn't undercook those pork chops. There shouldn't have been anything at supper to upset his stomach. I had the same food, and I felt fine.

"Honey, let me drive." I held out my hand, palm up.

He handed me the keys without any fuss. When we got home, he undressed and climbed into bed before I told him to.

"I don't want any . . . darn . . . Pepto Bismol, Carolyn. I'm fine. I simply need to rest for awhile. I think my stomach is doing better already." He put his glasses next to the lamp and set the alarm clock, a sure sign he wouldn't be joining me to watch TV later.

Darrell had been retired for six years now, but he still set that alarm for 6:15 every night. I had no idea why. You'd think the man would enjoy sleeping late now and then.

I couldn't find anything worth watching on the television, so I ended up reading *The Other Side of Midnight* until I couldn't hold my eyes open any more, right about midnight, I noted with irony. I could hear Darrell snoring softly in the bedroom before I got to the end of the hallway. I climbed into bed as gently as possible, careful not to disturb him. After a few minutes, I curled myself around his warm back and fell asleep, my legs pressed into his.

The alarm buzzed as usual, and I hoped, for the thousandth time, he would turn it off and go back to sleep. Instead, he stretched and swung his feet around into his slippers. I refused to open my eyes, but asked him, "How is your stomach?"

"Better, I think."

He shuffled off down the hall, and I rolled over, flipping my pillow to the cool side. I must try to get the man to stay up later with me at night; it's my only chance to sleep until a decent hour.

The next thing I knew, it's 8:12 and I could hear Darrell mowing out back. The neighbors had to hate the noise at that time of morning, though I guessed everyone in the neighborhood was up. I sighed and threw on my robe, making a mental note to remind Darrell that the Jenkins had a new baby. Those poor people might just be getting to sleep.

I poured my second cup of coffee when the noise finally stopped. I could hear Darrell trying to re-start the mower in the front yard. It didn't sound like he was having much success. As I flipped through the newspaper, I heard him come in through the front door. I looked up to find him clutching his left arm, his face frozen in pain.

"Honey?" he managed to say.

His legs gave way in slow motion, and he was on his knees. God, no. God, please no. I ran to him, trying desperately to know what to do. He seemed to be losing consciousness.

"Darrell? Darrell!" I screamed. I ran to the kitchen phone and dialed 9-1-1, just like the new sticker said.

"I think my husband is having a heart attack. Please send an ambulance. Please hurry. Please!"

Darrell had rolled over onto his side.

"What is your address, ma'am?"

I was shaking so violently I thought I was going to drop the phone. "It's 383 Highlands Avenue. Please, please hurry!" I threw the phone down and ran back to my husband, cradling his head in my lap. "Please, Honey, please, hang on. The ambulance is coming.

You're going to be fine. You're going to be fine, Darrell." I realized I was rocking back and forth.

Darrell groaned. He was still with me.

"Please, Darrell, please. Breathe, honey." He was sweaty. Drenched. Oh, God, please.

It seemed like forever until I finally heard the sirens. Then the emergency medical men were running in the front door.

I was yelling, "In here! In here!" I jumped up to let them save my husband. I could only stand there, a helpless lump, while they pounded on Darrell and put an oxygen mask on him and hooked him up to some sort of equipment.

"Ma'am? Did you hear me?" The young one was speaking to me.

"I'm sorry, what?"

He put his hand on my arm. "Ma'am? We have him stabilized now. We're taking him to Hudson Medical Center." He glanced at my robe. "Do you have a neighbor who can drive you there?"

"Yes. No. I'll drive myself."

They were loading my husband onto a stretcher. They were carrying him out the front door. Clothes. I needed to get dressed. I ran upstairs and threw on a dress, then ran to the car. I couldn't find the keys, Darrell, where are the keys? I remembered I drove last, so they're in my purse. Dear God, please let him be all right.

The lady at the desk in the emergency room could see my panic. She immediately launched into calm the family mode. "Yes, ma'am. Can I help you?"

"Yes. They brought my husband here. Darrell Parker."

"He's with the doctor now, ma'am. If you'll have a seat, I'll let you know when you can go back there." She smiled; a reassuring, we-are-doing-everything-we-can smile. "It will only be a few more minutes, I'm sure. Dr. Forbes will be out to talk to you, or I'll take you back."

Ellen. I should call Ellen. "Can you tell me where I could find a pay phone?"

"You can use this phone on the counter, Mrs. Parker."

Ellen was Darrell's daughter, from his first marriage. She was already in her teens when Darrell and I married, and while we had been close at times, I had been more like an older aunt to her than a second mother. I had been grateful for even that, because I knew Margaret told her daughter how Darrell and I got together in the first place, and about the divorce. She was married, too, with a son of her own. Tommy was a beautiful little boy with warm brown eyes and a smile that could light up a room. I prayed to God to please let Darrell watch his grandson grow up. Tommy was only three.

"Ellie? This is Carolyn. It's your dad, Ellie. He's fine right now, but I think he had a heart attack. We're at Hudson Medical Center."

Ellen would be there in twenty minutes. I swore I would never let the man eat bacon again if God let this be a warning.

I could not sit down. I was sure it annoyed the other people waiting, but I had to stand. I tried to stand in the corner, by the window. When I couldn't be still for one more second, I paced. There was a little girl with her hand wrapped in gauze, crying intermittently while her mother comforted her, wiping tears with her thumb. There was a young couple, a tiny baby sleeping in the girl's arms; an elderly man near the television coughing violently and looking scared. We all looked scared.

"Mrs. Parker?"

Here was the man with my whole life in his hands. This was bad. They should have been calling me back, not sending the doctor out with news. I walked over to him, trying to prepare myself. He extended his hand to hold—not shake—mine.

"Mrs. Parker, I'm Dr. Forbes. Your husband has suffered a massive myocardial infarction. A heart attack. I'm going to walk you back to be with him in a minute, all right?" He searched my eyes.

"Mrs. Parker, we have done everything we can for your husband at this point. We need to run some more tests to assess the damage to his heart muscle, and we'll be doing that soon. In the meantime," he smiled, kindness in his eyes, "I know he wants you by his side. Please follow me."

Darrell was behind a white curtain, his bed elevated a bit, but mostly lying down. I started to fall to pieces as soon as his eyes met mine. I was not brave. I had never been brave.

"Hi." I sat down in the orange plastic chair by his bed. "You gave me quite a scare."

"Scared myself, too, honey. Scared myself pretty good. I'm feeling much better now, Carolyn. I love you."

I couldn't help it. Any semblance of cool, calm and collected was out the window. I sobbed, "I love you, too. Don't you ever, ever do that to me again. I don't want to live without you, Darrell Parker. I don't." The tears flowed freely now. I couldn't stop them for anything. He stroked my hair. I was not doing a very good job of comforting my husband.

"Shh. I'll be fine, Carolyn. I will be fine." His voice was so weak. I just sat there, unable to look up. I didn't want to upset him more with my tears.

"Hi, Ellie," Darrell said.

I hadn't heard her walk in. I jumped up and hugged her, then moved out of the way. Suddenly, I felt like I was intruding. "Honey," I said, "I'm going to go freshen up a bit. I'll be back in a few minutes."

Darrell smiled and made a little wave. Ellie took my place in the chair.

When I got back, a nurse was there.

"We're going to take Mr. Parker for some tests. He'll be back in about an hour."

Ellen and I kissed Darrell, one on each side of his forehead.

"I love you two," he said. "I'll be back soon." Like he was controlling this. Like he has always controlled everything; he had always been capable, in charge. What if I have to live without him? I wondered. I didn't know where to begin. Ellen said, "Carolyn, come sit down here. Please."

But I preferred to stand. "What happened?" Ellen asked. "What was he doing? What did the doctor say?"

Suddenly, Reverend Gleason was in the doorway. How did he hear about Darrell?

"Carolyn. I came as soon as I heard."

I didn't care how he heard. I felt disconnected from my body.

"The nurse said they've taken him for tests. It was his heart?"

"Yes, Larry, it's his heart. We're waiting to find out more. This is Darrell's daughter, Ellen. Ellen, this is Reverend Larry Gleason."

Just then, Dr. Forbes came in. "Mrs. Parker, we're going to need to do surgery. I'm afraid the damage to Mr. Parker's heart was extensive. They're prepping him now."

Now? I didn't even get to kiss him, to reassure him.

"The waiting room for the OR is on the fourth floor. I'll meet you there as soon as the operation is over."

Reverend Gleason took my hand. I did not want him to take my hand. Hand-holding was for women whose husbands were going to die. I pulled away, excusing myself to the ladies' room, "I'll meet you two in a few minutes."

Our wait was cruelly, horribly short. Dr. Forbes took my hand, just like Larry did. I didn't want him to, either. The rest was a blur. They let me kiss Darrell a final goodbye. I went home. I called the funeral home. I did a thousand things new widows do. I made no pretense of strength. I leaned on my closest friends, the oldest and dearest of whom, Betsy, went out and bought me a new black dress. I received casseroles from my sweet neighbors.

Ellen and her husband, Tom, sat beside me at the funeral. I was so grateful Ellen was with me; she was as close as I would ever have to a daughter of my own. Darrell and I wanted children, but I could never get pregnant. She was crying off and on. I put my arm around her. She made the right decision, I thought, having Tommy stay in the nursery. He came to church with us occasionally; knew Mrs. Wilson. Reverend Gleason talked about Darrell's life, his practice, his many friends, his faith in God. He assured Ellen and me, "You will join Darrell in Heaven someday."

I was glad to see people pay their respects; many of them drove from far away. Darrell's first wife, Margaret, and her husband Carl walked up. She kissed me on the cheek and told me, "I am very sorry, Carolyn."

After the burial service, Ellie, Tom and I came back to the house, where Betsy had set out food for everyone. Visitors were already there, waiting for us with hugs and stories of Darrell. We laughed about the time he brought in live animals for the annual outdoor nativity scene, and somehow managed to secure a camel. The thing spit on him every time he came close.

I kept thinking how much he would have loved the banana pudding.

It had been a month, and I kept reliving that week, especially Sunday and Monday. Wondering if I should have seen the signs earlier. If I should have gotten Darrell to a doctor. The man had to be dragged in for any kind of medical attention; I probably couldn't have persuaded him to go.

I gave the lawn mower, the murderous lawn mower, to the Jones boy down the street. He would mow our lawn from then on. I went through all of Darrell's things and donated his clothes to the Salvation Army. Tucked away in a Vanderbilt University yearbook, I found a secret. It was a letter he wrote to Margaret in 1937, unfolded, uncreased, unsent for whatever reason. He wrote about his visit with her the week before. He went on and on about her hair and eyes and a green swimsuit he liked on her. He told her he would be home soon, and he wanted to marry her. He wanted them to have three beautiful daughters, looking like her, and a son. He wanted to come home to her every night.

I put it in an envelope and mailed it to Margaret. I couldn't throw it away, and I thought—I hoped—it would mean something to her.

The Country Sky Is Different
Lily

The man walked by every morning with six dogs trotting ahead or alongside him. Each of them was different: there was a big black fluffy one, a beagle-ish hound, a German Shepherd mix, a little brown rat-looking mutt, a huge tan thing that looked like a sheepdog, and a fat little Chihuahua. It's the oddest parade I've ever seen. None of them were on leashes, so I didn't think he was one of those professional dog walkers. I couldn't imagine that out in the country, anyway. They were on the road that ran east by the house; the highway would never accommodate that kind of procession. They came right up to the corner, then turned around and went back to wherever they came from. He was wearing his big floppy hat, safari pants and carried a walking stick. Looked more like he was off to climb a mountain than walk his dogs.

"Millard, look at this. Have you seen this crazy white man with his dog parade?"

Millard grunted, "No," and turned the newspaper page.

Daniel and his dog, Rocket, hadn't been out when they passed by. Rocket would probably have tried to take off and run with them, though he had been good about staying in the fenced yard.

My Daniel was finally getting used to our new home, far from the neighborhood he had memorized, right down to the number of steps to the corner convenience store. Daniel was special; he was slower to learn than most people. He would be thirty in a few years, and he lived very happily with his daddy and me. He was full of love for everyone he met. He was the greatest blessing in my life. God only picks a few people to get to keep their children's hearts close at home with them, safe and protected from the evil in this world. Moving out there was mostly about protecting Daniel. There were too many bad things going on in our old neighborhood. Too many crazy young boys bent on showing the world they could use a gun like a man. They didn't have the first idea what being a man is about.

Daniel knew never to leave the yard, Daniel knew not to talk to strangers. Still, it was all new to him, and I worried that he would forget, or decide to test my limits.

My older son, Todd, thought I kept Daniel too sheltered; Daniel's closest friends in the world were me, his father, and his brother. I didn't think that's such a bad thing. It wasn't possible for him to socialize where we used to live.

Todd nagged me, "Momma, take him to the Sunshine Day Center in town. He would enjoy it."

That's where they'd put him in a room with others like him and teach them to make things out of popsicle sticks. I thought Daniel was very happy spending his days with me, and, since his retirement, Millard.

I worry about my Millard, too. His hip kept getting worse, and he used his cane almost all the time now. The doctors didn't seem to be able to do anything to help, and I knew my husband was scared he was going to be seated permanently in some chair, with me and Daniel rolling him around. He wouldn't go to church.

"Lily," he said, "My hip is hurting too much."

Daniel and I went alone, and it was a long drive from out here.

I was peeling my sixth potato at the sink when Daniel entered the kitchen, Rocket at his heels.

"Momma, I wanna do my telescope today."

"I'll help you, Daniel. But we need to wait until later to set it up, after supper, and then until it gets very dark outside to look through it."

The telescope was as much for me as for Daniel. Out in the country, I figured we would be able to see a lot of things in the night sky that were hidden in town, with all the lights around. I taught sixth grade science for years—long enough to have to re-learn things over, with the new discoveries in the world. When I started, the children were making models of the solar system with Pluto on the longest coat hanger wire, and that's about what we covered. Then we put a man on the moon. There are space shuttles going back and forth to a manned space station. Exploring Mars. The new textbooks have pictures from the Hubble telescope, reaching out into the universe. It amazed me.

One of my brightest students ever, John Payne, worked at Marshall Space Center in Huntsville. When he was with me, he won the National Science Fair with a project on the desalination of water. He became a rocket scientist, the real thing. Imagine that, one of my kids engineering the vehicles that the whole world watches in awe. He called me the day after they lost the Columbia. It was the saddest day of that boy's life.

"Okay, Momma. Me and Rocket are going out back."

"Rocket and I."

Rocket shot me a look as he trotted by. I swear that dog could grin. He had been a good companion for Daniel, and hardly any trouble.

After supper, I took the telescope parts out of the box and placed them on the kitchen table for my husband to assemble. It was my job to read the instructions—Millard would be offended at the idea he ever actually needed instructions to put anything together—and find answers if Millard had a question. I knew better than to volunteer information about this bolt or that screw. It was also my job to keep his cussing to a minimum when things didn't fit together right.

When it got dark enough, Daniel and I carried the telescope and its stand outside, and I set it up in the middle of the back yard. It was a brilliant night, cool, crisp and calm. The sky was black velvet studded with a million diamonds, some huge, some barely twinkling at us. Daniel gasped, his head lolled back on his shoulders.

When I figured out how to adjust the focus, I decided we'd start with the moon.

"Look, son, this is the moon. Can you believe men walked around up there, years ago? Look at the big craters."

We moved on to Jupiter, and then Saturn. Daniel particularly liked Saturn's rings.

"Daniel, look at this. It's the star called Castor. And this one, I swung the scope a bit, "is Pollux."

Every single time I stepped aside to let my son look, he yelled, "Wow!" I was pleased that he enjoyed this so much. Almost too much. Many stars and planets later, I told Daniel, "We have to go inside. I promise we'll come back out tomorrow night." We left the telescope where it was. Daniel patted it a fond goodnight.

At 6:18 a.m., I was awakened by dogs, barking, yelping, and howling. It sounded like twenty of them. I threw my housecoat on and ran to the kitchen window. The dog parade man was out by our fence, dancing around, trying to shove his dogs back. He was using his leg, his walking stick, elbow; whatever he could push with. He looked desperately in need of help. I paused for an instant, and then ran outside.

"Do you have a sudbell?" he yelled. I stood there, confused. I could only hear barking.

"Do you have a shovel?" He pantomimed, digging a trench for me. Very helpful.

I ran around to Millard's tool shed and grabbed the only shovel I saw. I ran toward him.

He screamed above the dog chorus, "Snake!" pointing at the ground.

I saw it—a long, fat snake, curled up by a post. Lord, I hated snakes. I was terrified, and froze for a few seconds. The snake, unwilling to engage six dogs, found an opening and shot off across the road. The poor man nearly killed himself holding back the pack, a tidal wave of fur and teeth. He waved, signaling that the fence line, for now at least, was serpent-free.

Millard and Daniel were at the edge of the porch. I heard Rocket, desperate to join the excitement outside, barking and howling in the house. Thank goodness Millard didn't let him follow Daniel.

I was outside in my housecoat and this man was walking around to our gate, letting himself in. I got up on the porch with my family, finger-combing my hair into place.

The dogs followed him in, oddly organized now into some kind of pecking order. Pack order. The fluffy black one looked like it must have been his favorite, right by his side. The rest trailed behind, and then sat themselves down, panting.

"Thought I should let you all know that was a rattler. About four feet long. He was coming from your back yard when the dogs stopped him."

Shoot, that snake was seven feet long if it was an inch. I moved to the swing, feeling faint.

"I'm Ben Perkins," he said, shaking Millard's hand.

"Millard Taylor. Nice to meet you. This is my son, Daniel, and my wife Lily." I waved shyly from the swing.

"I saw that you folks had moved in here. Nice to have somebody in this house, finally. Welcome to the neighborhood."

We have a neighborhood? We are at least a quarter mile from the nearest house.

"Thank you, Mr. Perkins. We'll keep an eye out." Millard smiled, leaning against the porch column.

Daniel said, "Thank you." Very serious, very official, like his dad.

Millard nodded at the pack. "You sure do have a lot of dogs."

Ben Perkins laughed. "I don't own a single one. My wife and I live down on the river," he nodded to the east, "and three of them, Brandy here, Belle and Rusty, seem to prefer our house to their own. The rest are stragglers we pick up as we go for our morning walk. I guess we make for quite a sight. My wife says I look like a shepherd with a bizarre flock."

"Do you want to see my Legos?" Daniel volunteered.

Son, I am sitting here in my housecoat, for Heaven's sake.

"Thank you, Daniel, but I'm going to have to herd these guys toward home. I'd sure like to see them another time, though. I promise. I love putting models together, but I've never worked with Legos."

My heart said: Thank you, Mr. Perkins. That was very kind.

"Before I forget," he said, turning to leave, "has Perry been by here yet?"

Millard glanced at me, and I shook my head. "No, we haven't met a Perry."

"Well, you will. No one can move in around here without a pitch from Perry about the fire department. Used to be my job last year. I figure you'll see him before long. Y'all have a good day!" When he reached the gate the dogs shot out like they were at a racetrack; maybe they were hoping the snake was back.

When we went back inside I started breakfast as Millard and Daniel watched from the kitchen table. I hated having an audience while I cooked.

"I am never going out in that yard again. Did you see that thing, Millard? Slithering around my house. Daniel, I want you and Rocket to stay in today."

"Lily, be reasonable. That snake's not gonna bother the boy. Snake's scared of him. Besides, Daniel, you'll watch out and be careful, right?"

Daniel nodded solemnly. "I know about snakes."

I shot Millard a dirty look. "Son, go wash your hands before breakfast," I said, waiting for him to leave the room, "Millard, we were out there barefoot last night. Scares me to death. You know as well as I do Daniel wouldn't know what to do if he came up on a rattlesnake." I shivered, and felt the skin on my arms crawl.

"He has the dog with him, Lily. Besides, no snake is going to seek him out. I'll talk to him; tell him to stay away from the heavy brush out back if you want me to. But don't be silly, woman. You can't keep him locked inside."

The rest of the day, I scanned the yard out the window over and over while Daniel was outside. Like the snake was going to wave and tell me he was out there, and I should come and get my son in the house.

"Lily," Millard says after we climb into bed, "Loosen up a little. Let the boy have some freedom. He's loving this out here, bein' able to explore." He rubs his thumb along my cheek, tilting my head up for a kiss. "You know it's good for him."

The following morning was my favorite kind, sleeping late. Daniel watched Saturday morning cartoons, slipping Rocket pieces of cereal when he thought I was not looking. I was stretched out on the couch with the paper, handing a section to Millard in his chair, when Rocket started growling. There was a knock at the door. I made a dash for the bedroom, determined that the neighbors were not going to believe I wear nothing but a housecoat. I glimpsed the slim window next to the door. Black man this time, early thirties.

I strained to hear while changing into a blouse and pants.

Millard said, "Come into the living room."

I heard "fire department" and realized this must have been Perry, fundraiser for this year. I looked for my purse. I was sure there's a twenty in there.

". . . the thing is, I have a bum hip, you know. Otherwise, I'd love to help y'all. Sure would." Millard was telling him.

"Well, what about Daniel, here? We have lots of jobs we need help with." Perry was looking at my son and gesturing.

I saw Daniel grinning, nodding energetically.

Millard bobbed his head the tiniest bit, eyebrows raised.

I rounded the corner, adjusting my collar.

"Lily, this is Perry; he's here from the volunteer fire department."

Perry shook my hand.

Oh. Oh, no, you're not, Millard Taylor, either. I turn to Millard, a false, tight smile on my face. "I don't think . . ."

Millard cut me off, a man living very dangerously. "I'm sure Daniel would like that, wouldn't you, son?"

What was he thinking? Daniel? Fighting fires? I would have to handle this after Perry left. Somehow. Daniel looked more excited than he was the day we brought Rocket home. Dammit, Millard.

"Yes!" Daniel looked at me, his eyes pleading.

I should have stayed in my housecoat and nipped this mess in the bud. "We'll talk about it later, son, okay?" I squeezed Daniel's shoulders from behind. "Perry, can I get you some coffee? A Coke?"

"No, thank you ma'am, I have to get going. Fire meeting's Monday night at seven, and Millard, you come along and sign up too, if you like. We'll find you a desk job, or something. You know how to get there?"

This young man did not notice I never said yes?

"Straight out 78, right?" Millard asked.

"Right. See y'all later, then." Perry smiled and headed for the porch, winking at Daniel.

I burned holes in Millard with my eyes, before the door was closed. "You know he can't be a fire department volunteer," I hissed under my breath.

"Lily, I know he can. Look, honey, they have jobs like helping roll the hoses out to dry after they're used, then rolling them back up. Keeping the engine clean. He might ride out on calls with them, but they won't let him get near any danger. It would be great for him, Lily. You saw how excited he was." He tilted his head toward Daniel, lost again in cartoons.

"I don't know those people, Millard. I don't know how they'd respond to him, how they'd treat him."

"Lily, I'd go to the meeting with him; check them out. You met Perry. He's a good man. Everyone works together out here."

I turned and stomped off to the bedroom. First, deadly snakes. Now, firefighting. It was safer with the gangs on Sixth Street.

"Momma?" Daniel whispered loudly at the closed door.

"Come on in, Son."

"I can help the firemen, Momma. I can do that. I can help when there's a fire."

"I know. It's just . . ."

He looked like he was going to cry. I felt like I was about to. "I'll think about it, Daniel."

"Me and Rocket are going out back."

"Okay." I was defeated. On grammar, on snake-in-the-yard safety, and they were trying to defeat me on keeping my baby away from flaming timbers falling on his head.

As soon as it was dark, Daniel expected me to go back out to the telescope. I put on my jeans and winter boots. I told him, "You have to wear your long pants and boots" even though it was at least seventy degrees. I turned on every outside light, whether it would interfere with star-gazing or not. I stomped my feet and talked loudly making my way out there. I made Millard sit near us in a lawn chair. Still, I worried about that snake.

We found Betelgeuse first and then, after a lot of effort, Arcturus. I pointed for Daniel, "Look, there are Castor and Pollux again, the twins."

Millard directed us, "Find Sirius, the Dog Star."

Daniel asked, "Momma, what does it mean to reach for the stars?"

"Where did you hear that?" I glanced at Millard, who was smiling at the ground.

"Daddy said ask you. He said you used to say it to your kids you taught."

"I did." I sighed. I am defeated by my own inspirational quote. "It means to try your best to do things you never thought you could."

Millard leaned forward, waiting. Nicely done, old man.

"And, well, I think you should go to the fire meeting with your dad Monday night. See what it's about."

"Yes!" Daniel grinned, clapped his hands and rocked from side to side, causing Rocket to bark excitedly. "I will be fine, Momma."

I arranged a smile on my face in the moonlight. "I know you will, son. I know you will." I glanced around for the snake, making sure Rocket wasn't barking at him.

The Hunger

Mary Kathleen—1849

Though it was still dark, I made my way to the tiny grave, a cairn of rough brown stones. I had been stopping there every day as I walked to work, to apologize, to weep, to pray. I tried to place a new wildflower between the rocks each time, especially daisies. Kieran loved to pull daisies apart, petal by petal. Sometimes I scattered the petals for him, my fine smiling baby boy, eyes dancing, heart of my heart.

He was not laid to rest in the churchyard, though we would have preferred that; we didn't have the money for a church burial. It was just as well with me; I had time with my son alone here, away from prying eyes. I could talk to him, and tell him that I still loved him so.

Would it ever end, this grief? It had been nearly five months, and it cut as deep each new day. I wish I had known to hoard food when the potatoes started dying. If only I had seen how Kieran was weakening, before it was too late. The blame would always be mine to carry.

I could imagine him running and playing in the field off to the east as I watched the sun rise. It was my signal to hurry on, and I leaned over and kiss the cool stones.

When I arrived, Oona nodded toward the fire and returned to stirring porridge. Oona was a good woman from Cork, and she pleased the Buxtons with her stews, roasts and puddings. It was her job to make sure it all tastes good, it was her great good fortune to sample bits as she cooks. She took full advantage, still managing to keep her figure somewhat rounded both for her husband, Pete the stable hand, and the tiny baby within her. None of us begrudged Oona her morsels of food, and we hoped her wee one would be born healthy. We wanted to see this new life as a sign that things would get better, refusing to dwell on the hunger that dogged, gnawing away. Food, any food, was our constant preoccupation. Some days, it was a dream we remembered in bits here and there—a bite of creamy pudding resting on the tongue; roast beef tender and savory, dripping juice.

Seamus and I were far luckier than most. We had lost my darling Kieran, but we had scraps from the Buxton kitchen some days to feed Patrick. He was thin, but strong. I pinched his arm most evenings, checking the flesh there.

He would swat my hand away. He tells me, "I'm fine, you shouldn't worry over me." The boy is barely seven years old, and he knew too much.

I prayed for Patrick's future, for the babies Seamus promised we would have.

I stoked the fire to Oona's satisfaction and assembled a tray for Eliza. She would be wanting her breakfast; there was no need of a bell for Eliza. She was as much a creature of habit as her father, Henry. Two fresh eggs, poached, with two strips of bacon. One slice of hearty bread, heavily buttered. Tea with cream and sugar—a feast that would have held my family well for a day. When I presented this to her, she did not even look my way. She directed me to the blue dress draped across her reading chair.

"It must be mended by this afternoon."

Her suitor was arriving, a pasty Army officer named Durham, posted in Kilkenny. He's nice enough, but Pete says he beats his horse with a whip. Pete said a man who will do that to a horse will likely do it to a woman, but Pete was overly fond of horses and exaggerations both.

As I was sitting in a corner of the kitchen with the dress, a curious thing happened. Lord Buxton came into the room, all disheveled. He said, "Oona, prepare extra stew and bread for a guest this evening." Oona glanced at me as he left, and gently lifted her shoulders. He had never entered the kitchen, at least not in our memories. Where was Lady Catherine? Was she ill?

We discover later that she was far from ill; she left with the head butler Sneed to return to London. Cora, the upstairs maid, has the details and they're interesting, indeed. She overheard Lady Buxton yell at her husband that she's ". . . sick of living in this primitive place with these illiterate people. I want our daughter to accompany me back to London. We're leaving at the first light of day."

Eliza was unwilling—no surprise there: she was ever her father's daughter.

We pondered this news, and its implications for us. I realized, sinking back onto the kitchen stool, that I was likely hit hardest. Eliza was the new mistress of Buxton House. That would either serve to elevate me or set off a fresh series of unkindnesses from a newly-empowered Eliza. The latter, I feared, was much more probable. I waited to see; what choice did I have in this world, anyway? It was foolish to speculate and worry.

I finished Eliza's dress after the noon meal was served, and she inspected it closely in the light of the drawing room windows, brushing her tight brown curls back from her forehead. Eliza was beautiful, I granted her due, but it was deceptive. Behind the smile and glittering brown eyes were a wicked temper and sharp tongue. My mother used to tell me that "pretty is as pretty does, Mary Kathleen." If that is the case, Eliza was a gargoyle, like the one I once saw on Saint Patrick's Cathedral in Dublin. It was surprising, then, that she thanked me for my fine needlework before dismissing me. I wondered if Eliza was trying on the role of kind mistress now that she was in charge.

When I mentioned that to Oona, she laughed aloud.

"You'll sooner see white blackbirds, girl."

When Captain Durham arrived, it was I who showed him to the parlor to await Eliza. Lord Buxton had disappeared, so the man sat alone. I offered, "Tea, or water perhaps?" but he declined with a curt, "No, thank you very much."

I was not sure I believed Pete—the captain seemed much more inclined to politeness than cruelty. I didn't like the way he eyed me like a bar maiden, though, and I held my head high as I exited the room.

Eliza seemed especially excited to see her beau; she had even applied rouge to her white cheeks. The blue dress looks well on her, and she was wearing her sapphire earrings. When she turned to descend the stairs, she stunned me by suggesting, "Mary Katherine, why don't you leave early today?" for the first time ever.

"Thank you" I said, and hurried to the kitchen, flaunting my good fortune at Oona.

She told me, "Stay out of trouble, lass" and secretly handed me a slice of venison and two hunks of carrot, wrapped in white cloth. I slipped it under my shawl and headed for home, eager to surprise Seamus and Patrick.

I found Patrick alone, because Seamus was off to shoe Mr. Neely's horse. Patrick inhaled the portion of food I gave him as I promised, "There will be more for supper." I searched for an onion; maybe we would enjoy our own stew tonight. I cannot remember a day this good in a long, long time.

Seamus discovered me digging in what was left of our tiny garden, smiling as I held a small, perfect onion for him to see. When he took me in his arms, he smelled of sweat and horse, but I didn't care. It was a tender moment. At the same time, though, our ribs pressed together—a disturbing reminder of how meager our circumstances had become. I sighed, telling my husband, "We'll have a nice supper tonight, thanks to Oona's help."

It was good, watching Patrick and Seamus eat. They required far more than I, and I made sure they got it. I said a prayer of thanks—"Lord, please continue to bless us"—before falling asleep, and told Kieran I miss him.

The next morning, the staff was assembled in Lord Buxton's huge library, and an announcement was made. "Eliza Buxton is betrothed to Captain Charles Durham, and wedding preparations will begin next week." Lady Buxton would be arriving from England in one month, in time for the ceremony. We wish Eliza, resplendent next to her father, much happiness as we filed out. She arranged her hair with her left hand, showing off the engagement ring—a huge diamond glinting in the early morning sun. It made tiny rainbows on Lord Buxton's prized leather-bound collection.

In the weeks that followed, the food shortage finally reached Buxton House; Oona couldn't get what she needed for her daily cooking, and feared "The wedding feast will be far less than it should." She skimped here and there, explaining as best she could to an angry Eliza that there was less and less meat to be had, and "good vegetables have grown scarce."

Eliza told us, "Do whatever is necessary to procure what is needed", but neither Lord Buxton or his daughter seemed to understand that money alone could not generate food. One morning, Oona received Eliza's untouched breakfast tray from me, followed by a lecture from my mistress about its inadequacy.

"Really, Oona, this was hardly edible."

Two weeks later, she was especially irritable when I served her tea. It seemed her engagement ring was too large; she had lost weight. She placed it on a gold chain to wear around her neck until it could be properly re-sized.

We stayed busy with ordering, planning and sewing, much of it done by me, including Eliza's silk wedding dress. This is followed by a whirlwind of cleaning, cooking and decorating. Guests were arriving. Lady Buxton sailed in two days before the wedding, accompanied by Sneed. She showed no emotion save for irritation at her husband. We saw the older Buxton children and their husbands and wives, all of whom lived in England.

When everything was in place for the ceremony, I was dismissed early once again. "Your services will not be required on this day." I was to return early tomorrow. Eliza would be away on her honeymoon, but Lady Buxton had assignments for me.

The next morning, however, the house slept for a long time. Oona and I awaited breakfast instructions.

Finally, Lady Buxton directed us, "Serve the guests in the dining room and then begin a general cleaning of the house." We hoped there would be leftovers, because we were offered no roast beef or bread from the wedding feast, not so much as a crumb of Oona's cake. We did not dare try to sneak anything past the head butler's watchful eye.

Hunger had taken its toll on me, but it was much worse for Oona. She had taken to sitting and resting whenever she could, and that was what she was doing when Lord Buxton interrupted our cleaning the library. Whether it was his wife or his recent lack of good fortune, I don't know, but something in him snapped.

He ordered Oona, his favorite cook, to "Leave immediately and never return." Just like that, she was banished. I dared not act as though I had taken notice; I simply continued to dust the books, staring hard at them.

When I left that night, it was with bread and bacon I had brazenly stolen on my way out. I stopped by Pete and Oona's to share it with them, to console poor Oona. I found her lying on their straw bed, nearly asleep. I try to force her to eat, but she would have none of it. She was no longer hungry. I told Pete, "Do your best for your wife; the baby needs food whether she wants it or not."

I stole something else, too, when Lord Buxton left the room—a tiny, original version of a book he prized. I figured it must be worth something, the way he regarded it. It was called *Gulliver's Travels*, and was bound in beautiful dark blue leather. It was a handsome little book; I wrapped it in my dusting cloth to protect and smuggle it. I placed it where no one would ever look—deep within a crack in the wall of St. Lazerian's Cathedral. You'd have to reach up to find it, and I was sure no one would. If my plan worked, it would be because of that book. I told no one except Seamus what I was thinking, but as it took shape, my idea seemed more and more like our best and only chance to survive.

Seamus and I tried to save every penny he earned from his smithing work, and I stole with more and more abandon from the Buxton kitchen. When Eliza returned with her new husband to pack her belongings and move to Kilkenny, I greeted her with a smile, knowing I would likely never see her hateful face again.

I was wrong, though, so very wrong. The next day, long before dawn, there was a violent knock at our door. The local sheriff, John Hayes, demanded to search our property. "You are accused of theft—theft of Eliza Buxton's diamond engagement ring." This came as a mighty surprise, as it was something I actually hadn't stolen. No mention was made of the little book, and I wondered if it had been missed. When Hayes finished tearing the room apart, he found nothing. The food I took was, of course, long gone. I was directed, "Accompany me to Buxton House immediately."

Eliza was furious, her face crimson. She and her father were standing on the lawn, and both had their arms folded across their chests; I could not help but think she's a perfect, female miniature of him.

She addressed me coldly, demanding, "Where is my ring?"

Of course I told her, "I have no idea."

I was ordered to leave then, warned that, "The search for the ring is not over. You should not set foot in this place again, or you will be arrested."

Late that night, Seamus and I took Patrick and visited Kieran's tiny grave, saying our final goodbyes with heavier hearts than imaginable. We crossed silently to the church and fetched the book, which I inserted into a secret pocket I had sewn in the folds of my dress. We set out on foot for Cobh, hoping to reach it in a few days, before we ran out of the things I had found for us to eat. Patrick slept with his head on his father's shoulder. I looked back at the church one last time, tears running down my face.

It took us four days, but we made it to the city, and did our best to buy cheap passage on a ship bound for America. We were surrounded by people far worse off than we were, people who were clearly dying. Seamus was turned away again and again; we didn't have enough money. We retreated to the woods and made a camp. I decided I had only one option, and the next morning, I walked to a jeweler in Cobh, and offered him my mother's slim gold band, the one I've worn as a wife for the past eight years. He paid me a pittance, a tenth of its worth, but it would be enough when combined with our meager savings. He kindly offered me a piece of bread, perhaps to sooth his conscience.

There we were: Seamus, Patrick and I on the first day of our voyage to America. I knew I would miss my home for the rest of my days, but I also knew my family would survive. And that was enough for me. To be sure, it was enough.

A Nice Visit

Lisa

I spotted Mother's mink collar before anything else. I was pretty sure it was the only one in the Birmingham airport today, as it was early October. She and Dad were looking left and right, anxiously seeking a familiar face, gauging the level of local civilization. It was their first trip south since our wedding in Atlanta, which was Southern, but still cosmopolitan enough for Mother.

They were still far away, the last to get off the plane because my dad refused to get into lines anywhere, ever. He would sit patiently as though his seat was the most comfortable spot in the universe rather than fall in behind his fellow passengers and wait. It made my mother crazy. With both of them retired, it seemed he had an entire new repertoire of irritating behaviors. They had been married forty-five years, and she said she was getting to know him all over again, one minute detail of Rush Limbaugh's show at a time.

I envisioned my mother carrying a red pen everywhere she went, and grading each human being she encountered. She taught high school English for many years, and Mrs. Larter had the well-deserved reputation of a very tough teacher—the kind you started out hating, gradually adjusted to, complained about constantly, and ultimately regarded as among the best you ever had. Dad was a few halls away, trying to instill knowledge of world history into the same students. He was more of a pushover, though. Even though Mother left Bryant Academy before he did, their last year's annual was dedicated to both of them, with side-by-side portraits; his smiling, hers somber.

Mother was truly a brilliant woman, and counted herself among the proto-feminists of the sixties. She supported women's lib, idolized Gloria Steinem, and would probably have been ensconced as a literature professor at the University of Chicago were it not for her propensity to bear children. I could see her illustrating the finer points of John Donne's writing for enraptured English Lit students. She was a bit of a Donne scholar, fascinated by the duality of his sensuous, scandalous poetry and his fiery sermons.

She was still pretty in her late sixties, with her hair dyed a soft brown. She wore huge sunglasses she probably bought at Field's. Her posture was regal and her manner reserved; a serene Borzoi to my dad's aging Labrador Retriever.

I was the fourth of their five children, all of us scattered to the wind around the United States, though I was the only one actually way out in the country, or below the Mason-Dixon Line. Delaney was their eleventh grandchild. I knew they adored her and they had enjoyed our visits to Chicago, but I think the grandparent novelty had worn off a bit. Delaney was the only child of an only child on Tommy's side, so it was a strong contrast in terms of spoiling and bragging.

They looked nervous, like they anticipated wayward deer hunters in the airport, drunkenly firing shots into the ceiling. I resisted the urge to greet them with beef jerky and Moon Pies.

Delaney insisted on putting both in my purse when we left the house.

They walked toward us now, bleary-eyed but energetic.

"Hello, Daddy. Welcome." I kissed him on the cheek and narrowly missed Mother's.

Delaney reached her chubby arms to encircle Mother's neck, my sweet charming baby girl. Her emotional maturity at four-and-a-half astounded me. Mother swung her over to hug, and it brought tears to my eyes. Mrs. Larter was not a hugger.

"Lisa, you look nice," my mother remarked. Since she was equal parts Mr. Blackwell and Jane Austen, I could easily interpret this. I looked dowdy and possibly plump in my long skirt and sweater.

"Delaney, I have a present for you," Mother said, handing her a pink bag. Inside was a small denim pocketbook with a heart made of silver sequins on the side.

"Thank you, Nana!" Delaney yelled. She couldn't have brought anything that would have thrilled her granddaughter more. "Mommy, can I put my Moon Pie in my new purse?"

I couldn't help it; I glanced nervously at my mother before snapping, "May I, Delaney. You know it's 'may'! And no, it's better if we leave it in my purse."

"What is a Moon Pie?" Dad inquired. Ah, the first step in Southern cultural literacy.

"I'll introduce you to them later, Dad. Probably too sweet for Mother, but you'll like them."

"Why don't you call me 'Mom', Lisa? 'Mother' is so formal." Where in the world did that come from? Since when?

Mom said, "Look inside, Delaney. There's a present for Beastie, too." Beastie was Delaney's little black Maltipoo, one of the cutest dogs ever created, basically fur-covered love. He was pushing two, but would forever look like a puppy. Mom brought a gourmet dog cookie from one of those bakeries like Woofgang Mozart.

Apparently, she was re-tooling her image in her retirement.

"Do you think he'll like it?" Mom asked.

"Yes, ma'am. Thank you." Delaney replied with a nod, examining her loot.

"Is there a ladies' room, Lisa?" Mom scanned the sides of the airport corridor.

"Right over there, Mother . . . Mom. We'll wait for you by the water fountain."

She looked puzzled. "Drinking fountain," I corrected.

Dad decided he would visit the men's room before the drive home. Good idea. They had no notion of the length of the trip, and it was going to surprise them.

"Is this your new car, Lisa?" Dad asked as we approached it in the parking garage. My new white SUV was two-toned, sporting red clay accents up about midway.

"Yes, Dad, it's a countrified Acura. I'm sorry I didn't get it washed for y'all, but it would look like this again a few hours later." I watched my mother's eyes slide toward me, incredulous. Y'all? I couldn't wait for an opportunity to say "all y'all" in front of her.

The truth was, I never, ever wanted to live out in the sticks, and I had slowly grown to love Alabama almost as much as my husband did. I woke to cool air sweeping up from the valley below and into our windows, and sometimes we watched the sun rise over the mountains from our warm, snug bed. There was almost no snow, and what we received was a treasured gift to play in. The sun shone bright most of the time, and the skies really were so blue.

I had met some great people, including Leila down the road. She read the same books I did, laughed at my jokes, and had natural warmth that drew everyone to her. We watched movies together and were thinking of starting a book club. The days were gentle and sweet when we were at home. I got enough trips into Birmingham to satisfy my shopping cravings. And like my parents might if they stayed long enough, I'd discovered that my preconceived notions were ridiculous. Lots of people regarded Tennessean Reese

Witherspoon as a traitor for participating in *Sweet Home Alabama.*
The stereotypes in that movie were absurd and unfair.

Dad selected the front seat, and Moth . . . Mom settled in next to
Delaney in the back, trying to fasten her car seat. I opened the door
next to my daughter, determined to head off a problem.

"Honey, we're not going to watch *Finding Nemo* on the way
home. You can talk to Nana instead."

Delaney looked up at me, wounded, but didn't fight.

Moth . . . Mom . . . Nana said, "I want to hear all about your
Maltipoo, Delaney. I've never met a Maltipoo. Does she do tricks?"

"He's a he, Nana. He can play dead if you yell, 'Bang!' I'll show
you. And he only goes potty outside."

"Well, that is very good."

I was trying to monitor their conversation, but Dad had lots of
questions.

"What time will Tommy be home? Does he still go fishing on
weekends? Do you like the Acura better than the Lexus? Did you
test drive the Lexus? Did you drive the Cadillac SUV?"

Mother said, "It's very pretty here, Lisa. The leaves have not
quite turned yet, but they will be lovely in a few weeks."

They have leaves in Chicago. I wanted her to notice the blue
mountains in the distance, the creek dancing over rocks beside the
road.

"We're almost there, Mom. When we turn, I'll show you the
lake."

Dad yawned and announced, "I'll be ready for a nap when we
get home."

Mom said, "The lake is nice." This woman with a vocabulary
allowing six zillion choices, who can do crossword puzzles in her
sleep. With her toes. "It's nice," she continued, "I'll bet they catch a
lot of fish in there."

I sighed and hoped the house impressed them. And it seemed to.

Mom called it "beautiful" and Dad said, "I'm looking forward to sitting by the huge bank of windows with binoculars trained across the valley."

I lit the logs Tommy had left strategically stacked for us in the fireplace; mostly for decoration, but it was a little chilly. Thank goodness he did that, because I was out of "magic logs". I needed grocery-store fire starters, or my blazes were all doomed to sizzle and fizzle. After they met Beastie, wiggling enthusiastic over new humans, I took them to their room.

"Oh, Lisa, thank you," Mom offered.

I had arranged pink roses, Mother's favorite, on the dresser in a Waterford vase. Her Andes Mints were in antique crystal dishes on each bedside table, and I was happy with the soft pink and green symphony of color. The new down comforter was the perfect paisley to match, and I had found the most gorgeous sage green velvet pillows with rose trim for the window seat. It was perfect with the deep cherry furniture and the Victorian-era watercolor floral above the bed. The sweeping view of Cheaha Mountain was spectacular.

"This is so nice." That word again.

I fired back: "I'll wake y'all for supper. Get some rest." I smiled and closed the door, hoping Mom remembered better adjectives in her sleep.

Delaney curled up on the couch with Beastie at her feet, watching Finding Nemo. We had a car copy and a living room copy. She fell asleep in a few minutes.

I checked on the pork tenderloin in the crock pot, which Leila assured me was foolproof. It smelled good. I mashed red potatoes, something I had mastered, and steamed green beans from Tommy and Delaney's garden. We had made chocolate cupcakes the day before, and they looked very appealing arranged on a three tiered porcelain stand. They smelled great, too. I cleaned a spot or two off the floor, but the kitchen was fine. I walked the house, straightening up, preparing for the grand tour.

Cooking was majorly stressful for me, so the following night, we were going to Lily and Millard's with Tommy's parents. They insisted on a cookout to say thank you for hauling their furniture to their new house, and the timing was perfect. Lily cooked like angels sing. We would sit at picnic tables, enjoying a gentle breeze, and Delaney could run around.

I heard Tommy drive up just as I heard someone coming downstairs. He was kissing me hello as Mother rounded the corner, embarrassed.

"No making out in the hall, kids."

Tommy gave her a shoulder hug and asked, "How do you like Alabama so far?"

"It's lovely, Tommy. Nice scenery." After more very small talk, he excused himself to change.

I heard Delaney chattering away as I headed back to the kitchen to work on our nice dinner. She would keep Mom busy for awhile. That would be nice.

I couldn't help it; after a bit, I had to eavesdrop. I had spent my life trying to know what my mother really felt, what she really held in her heart. Maybe she would tell her granddaughter. More likely, though, my four-year-old would be diagramming sentences by the time we got to the table.

I heard Mother telling her, "He's saying that the lady is so beautiful and so wonderful, even the fish in the river all want to crowd around her instead of swimming away. Can you imagine how special he thinks she is?"

Delaney's tiny voice intoned, "Come live with me . . ."

". . . and be my love, and we will some new pleasures prove, of golden sands and crystal brooks, with silken lines and silver hooks. There will the river whispering run, warmed by thine eyes more than the sun, and there the enamored fish will stay, begging themselves they may betray."

I walked into the living room, reciting: "When thou wilt swim in that live bath, each fish, which every channel hath, will amorously to thee swim, gladder to catch thee than thou him."

Mom looked up, smiling. "We were talking about fishing."

"It's never too early to sneak in a little Donne, Mom."

"I'm surprised you remember, Lisa. Do you know the entire poem?"

"Of course I do. All your children do. We spout sonnets at people in the grocery store." I winked at Delaney and sat at her feet, tugging on a tiny bare toe. "Supper will be ready in about thirty minutes. Do you think we'll have to wake Dad?"

"We might. He's quite fond of his naps, and reluctant to rejoin the world sometimes."

"I am not. The world just has to be interesting," Dad called as he came down the stairs. "I thought I heard Tommy."

"You did, Dad. He'll be joining us in a minute. Would you like a beer, or a glass of wine?"

"Do you have light beer?" Dad glanced at Mother, expecting brownie points for being health-conscious.

"I'm sorry, Dad; I think it's regular. Is that okay?"

He glanced at her again, defiantly. "Yes, Lisa, that will be even better. Might as well live it up on vacation." He settled in on the other side of Delaney as I walked to the kitchen.

Tommy joined me a minute later, looking for wine glasses.

"Mom wants wine?"

He nodded yes, eyes wide in exaggeration. He carried drinks aloft on a round tray, serving with a flourish. This was the first time in memory I sipped wine with my mother.

After dinner, which Mom pronounced heavenly—credited to red wine—we showed them the rest of the house and then went for a long tour around the property. Tommy had carved lots of trails through the woods; it was easy walking. The temperature had dropped, though, so we returned to watch TV for awhile. To watch *Finding Nemo*, which Delaney cajoled her grandparents into viewing. After she was tucked in, we broke out the popcorn and put a grown-up movie in; Dad liked George Clooney, I liked George Clooney, so it was *Oceans Eleven*.

Before we went to bed, Tommy asked, "Dad, would you like to take the boat out and fish tomorrow?"

Dad looked like he was ready to go at that moment. They headed out at seven o'clock the next morning. Mom and I slept late, had lunch and went to Delaney's ballet class in Birmingham. We planned to reconvene at five o'clock to go to Lily's.

Lunch was at Delaney's very favorite place—a frilly, feminine tearoom in Mountain Brook. She loved the beautifully presented tiny sandwiches and the desserts, especially mini éclairs, lemon meringue and pecan pie tarts, and teeny crystal cups filled with chocolate mousse or vanilla pudding. Ninety percent of the diners had iced sweet tea, but my mother, the closet colonial, ordered her own pot of Earl Grey.

We stood at the big window thirty minutes later, watching Delaney twirl clumsily with nine other little girls.

"She is so precious, Lisa. So beautiful. You are doing a magnificent job with Delaney," Mom said.

I felt the tears welling up. My mother could reduce me to a six-year-old so easily. "Thank you, Mom. I know it's not what you planned for me. I know I'm the underachiever. First, the pageants, which I know you hated. Then, Karen is a pediatrician, Laura teaches English, Danny is an attorney, and Lena has her little boutique. I'm just a mom. I am not exactly the successful daughter of a feminist."

"What in the world are you talking about, Lisa? The women's movement was about choice; about equal opportunities for all of us, yes, but more about the freedom to pursue our choice of career. And don't think for a minute that motherhood is the least of the careers you can select. It's the most difficult. I couldn't devote myself to it full-time."

My mouth hung open slightly. These were true revelations from Anne Larter. "I am not sure I understand, Mom. I thought you chose to continue teaching all those years."

"The tuition remission at Bryant was nice. We wanted you to have the best education we could provide. But I would've taught anyway, Lisa, because I never had the patience to be home when all of you were little. Children were always easier for me to deal with when they turned sixteen or so. You may recall, I taught summer school, even when your dad didn't." She stiffened slightly, clearly uncomfortable. "Look at her swinging her hair; those long golden curls." She smiled. "Was Tommy's hair like that?"

"Exactly. I'll show you pictures. He looked like a Gerber baby, only with pretty blond curls. Girly hair, because Ellen refused to cut it. She dressed him only in blue until he was five, and strangers would still compliment her "beautiful daughter"."

"Good thing he turned into a manly man."

"I certainly think so." I raised my eyebrows and grinned the most lasciviously I could manage.

After they made their final curtsy to Miss Elaine, Delaney ran to her Nana's arms. Mom carried her out, though I knew she was way too heavy.

Dad and Tommy weren't back when we drove up, and it was almost four. Either they were catching fish like crazy, or they had boat trouble. I tried Tommy's cell, but I got voicemail. We women started getting ready, and hoped the men got back early enough to shower.

Either that or we were taking separate cars. I was not riding with eau de worm.

About the time Mom, Delaney and I emerged, beautiful and trailing clouds of perfume, Tommy and Dad strolled in. Tommy insisted they would be in my car, smelling good, at five o'clock in fifteen minutes. And they were.

When we pulled into the driveway, Daniel was sitting on the

front steps, wearing his fireman's helmet. He had been volunteering at the local fire department, the greatest joy in his twenty-six years. He ran to the car, helping Mom out her side. When Delaney was extricated, he invited her to play with Legos.

"Don't put them in your mouth, Delaney," I yelled at her back. "I won't."

Lily and Millard were on the porch, along with Tommy's parents, Tom and Ellen. Everyone had met before, though Lily and Millard only knew my folks from our wedding. Lily ran inside and returned with a tray, offering, "Sweet tea or muscadine wine?"

Mom and I couldn't resist the exotic.

"Ooh, that's sweet," Mom whispered to me. We confined ourselves to teeny sips.

The men went around back to supervise the barbecue and speak about manly things; Mom and Lily settled on the front porch swing and Ellen and I got the chairs. I could spy Daniel and Delaney on the living room floor. He was patiently building tall towers, and she was gleefully knocking them down. Daniel's dog, Rocket, was helping with the demolition.

Predictably, the talk turned to teaching. Lily taught sixth grade science forever. I tuned in and out, more interested in Delaney's giggles.

Mom was telling Lily, "Teachers can never be paid enough for the work they do."

Lily responded with a nod and "Thank you."

A few minutes later, Mom bemoaned "the absolute ignorance of grammar and spelling in today's youth."

Another, more vigorous nod and "Thank you," from Lily.

After about twenty minutes, Millard yelled to his wife. "Lily! Y'all come on out here."

She shot off to the kitchen, refusing any offers of help. "No, everyone please find a place for themselves. I'll be right there."

Next, we heard the dinner bell out back. "It's tolling for us, Mom," I grinned.

They had pushed two tables together, and there was a long line of red and white flower arrangements down the center—so beautiful. Though it wouldn't be dark for hours, there were candles in hurricane globes between each one, already flickering atop red and white checkered tablecloths. Lily had outdone herself.

Millard offered a prayer, "Lord, thank you for family, for dear friends, for this food I've worked so hard to prepare."

Lily stuck her tongue out and rolled her eyes at him as we looked up.

The meal was incredible. Tender pulled pork barbecue in a tangy sauce—Lily's secret—piled inside home baked rolls, barbecue chicken breasts and pork ribs, sweet corn on the cob, spicy baked beans in a huge old pot, and a wonderful potato salad. For dessert, there was Lily's luscious homemade peach ice cream, filled with peaches from their own trees. It was, quite possibly, the best meal I had ever eaten. We lingered over every morsel, savoring the flavors.

We were talking, mostly about Tommy's teenage adventures, as it started to get dark. "Do you remember that last game he played in high school?" Millard winked at Tommy's dad.

Daniel and Delaney were chasing lightning bugs, squealing with delight. Rocket had been banished for begging, but Lily allowed him out after supper. He joined the chase, snapping at every bug he saw.

"Did I ever tell you," Ellen said, "that when I was a girl, we would catch lightning bugs and feed them to the goldfish in our pond? The fish would light up with a beautiful glow under the water. It was the neatest thing."

At first, no one believed her. Tommy had heard this story before, and was not sure it was true. Ellen insisted, eyebrow arched, "They looked like lanterns."

We all bought it, conjuring images of her pond filled with luminous golden fish, gracefully gliding under the dark surface.

Lily fetched the inevitable mayonnaise jars, so Delaney and Daniel could have insect-powered "night lights."

Lily accepted no help with the clean-up. "I'll pack up leftovers for everyone." There were hugs and back pats, and I noted that my mother was cheerfully hugging right along. We promised to get together again soon. I heard Lily reminding Mom, "Mail me that magazine article."

When we were about a minute into our ride home, my mother said, "This was the perfect Southern evening." Then I heard her mutter, "Catch a falling star . . ." from the backseat.

"What's that, Mom?"

"Oh, I just noticed "Stars Fell On Alabama" on that truck's license plate. It made me think of a Donne poem."

Of course it did.

She continued, "You live in a beautiful, friendly, magical place, Lisa and Tommy. I envy you."

That was a really nice thing for her to say. I was glad they came to visit.

A Chance Meeting, In Three Parts
Carla, 7:05 - 8:43

"We're trying to think of a new fundraiser. I suggested "A Chair-ity Ball", where we could have local celebrities auction off deck chairs they have decorated. The deck chair thing goes well with gardens. We would have it at the park, of course. Thousands of tiny white lights in the trees. It would be next Spring, when everything is blooming. What do you think?"

"I think that dress is dangerous." Evan appeared behind me in the mirror and hugged me, sliding his hands up my belly until I swatted him when he got too far north.

"We're going to be late as it is, you lecherous man." I got my left earring in, and turned to my husband. "Do you really like the dress?"

"I love the dress, Carla. Can't you tell I love the dress?" He eyed me up and down and up again, and addressed his comments to my breasts.

"Do you think A Chair-ity Ball would be good?" Evan was a partner in an ad agency; he usually had good input on these things.

"What celebrities do you have in mind?"

"I don't know. Maybe a news anchor or two from the local stations. The mayor. Courtney Cox Arquette. Condoleeza Rice."

"You're kidding, right?"

"Okay. Local news personalities. The mayor. City council-people. But I'll bet," I said as I handed him my car keys, "you could get me a real celebrity. You know big shots in Birmingham. Help us raise money to purchase new plants for the botanical gardens and purchase fertilizer. Help the starving plants. I'll bet Courtney or Condi would help feed the starving plants, if you'd get my foot in the door, Evan. You love my foot."

"I like your foot okay. I don't know their people, Carla. I can't even have my people call their people. Is the sitter here yet?"

"Yes, they're in the den watching TV and eating popcorn. I got Savannah." Savannah was Jacob's favorite babysitter. I think he had a crush on her.

"Let's get this over with." He reached over to turn out the bedroom light, sighing deeply. "I want to be home in time for the *Tonight Show*. Jennifer Love Hewitt is going to be on."

"Jennifer, huh? I bet you love her feet. I bet you'd get her foot in the door with Courtney."

"She has feet? I never noticed."

I smacked his butt with my evening bag.

The house—mansion, really—was a sight to see, with a zillion golden lights around the edges and throughout the grounds. Huge fir wreaths hung from the front doors, each festooned with gold ribbons, and there were smaller matching ones in every window. The massive white columns had the same lights embedded in their garlands, wrapped around. Those were topped with extravagant bows. I noticed that the tuxedoed valets had gold cummerbunds and ties—a nice touch.

Evan mused, "They went with understatement this year. I like it."

I knew he wouldn't be able to refrain from making some kind of crack. I thought it looked pretty, in a Disney World sort of way.

Doug and Junie Crandall greeted us in the grand foyer with hugs

and kisses. I'd worked for Mr. Crandall for several years in one of
the oldest and largest accounting firms in the city. Their annual
Christmas party, for both clients and employees, was legendary.

"Carla, you look beautiful, as always," Mrs. Crandall said, "and
Evan, you are a handsome devil in that tuxedo." I swear Mrs.
Crandall had someone holding up flashcards with names behind us.
Once a year, one hundred and fifty guests, and she would hit every
name. "You two know where everything is; drinks in the drawing
room, buffet in the dining room. Y'all have fun."

Mingling is mostly done in the great room, which is really a
ballroom, I think, with furniture arranged throughout. I settled into
a velvet couch, and batted my eyelashes at Evan. "Will you please
get me a glass of champagne?"

He scampered off obediently.

"I love your bag! Did you get it at Parisian?" I closed my purse
and looked up to see a very pretty woman, thirty-ish. I had no idea
who she was. Brunette, blue eyes. Was she the new associate's wife?
The shoes were either Christian Louboutin, or excellent knockoffs.
Was she married to the Cadillac dealer? Was she here with Dr.
Randolph, famed for being seventy but never dating above thirty?
She was not from the area. The accent was wrong. About the time I
decided I didn't know her, she introduced herself.

"Lisa Robinson. My husband is a client of Larry Hoffman's." She
plopped down next to me and ever-so-slowly removed her feet
from the gorgeous shoes, watching the whole time to see if anyone
was looking.

I noticed that along with her deep green silk gown she was
wearing a bracelet made of dyed macaroni, and each piece had
several rhinestones glued on.

"Do you like it?" she smiled brightly. "My daughter made it for
me, for tonight. Her name is Delaney."

"I love the bracelet, and I love the name. Delaney. How pretty.

I'm Carla Hansen. I'm a junior associate with Crandall, Lewis, Deaton & Hoffman. I work with Mr. Crandall, actually."

"Do you have children?"

"We have a son, Jacob. He's ten. If he made me a bracelet, it would be of frog pelts. Or dried tadpoles."

"You should watch Vogue carefully. Frog could be the new black."

I liked this woman.

"Do you live in Birmingham?"

She smiled. "No, I live in the middle of nowhere, perched high on a hill, surrounded by kudzu. But I'm in town a lot. Delaney has classes. I have shopping." She wiggled her half-on shoe daintily.

Evan returned, carefully carrying two flutes of champagne.

"Lisa, this is my husband, Evan. Evan, meet Lisa Robinson."

Lisa extended her hand, and I couldn't help but think it looked like she expected it to be taken and kissed, or at least clasped elegantly. Evan, clueless, shook it vigorously. I loved Evan for that.

"Hi, Evan. My husband disappeared into the buffet line eons ago. Did you see a man standing in front of a chafing dish with a fork, having dinner?"

"No, but I was in the drawing room. What is a drawing room, anyway?"

Lisa and I glanced at each other and replied in unison, "I have no idea."

The man who had to be Lisa's husband walked up, plate carefully balanced in hand, two forks. "I got us an assortment, honey. The drinks are in a different room." He turned to Evan and me. "Hi. I'm Tommy Robinson."

"Hi, Tommy, I'm Carla, and this is my husband, Evan."

Tommy was a good-looking man, though not the type to enjoy wearing a tux. I guessed he would be much happier in jeans, like Evan. Once they launched into a discussion of their connections to the Crandalls, I gently interrupted, "Please excuse me. I'm going to the powder room." Powder room. It was bigger than our bedroom. I wanted to check my face; women like Lisa Robinson made me a little bit insecure. I looked closely. Color's good, foundation's not too shiny. No mascara smudges. I still loved my eyes, and I was not sorry I had them done. No one would suspect I was forty-two. Dr. Clarke made me look prettier than I did in my twenties—possibly ever. My mom subtly suggested one time that my eyes looked different, but Evan's never said anything. Evan rarely looked above my boobs. I re-applied my lipstick, and smiled at the mirror.

Lisa, 8:47 - 8:56

That was fast. She didn't have to go pee. She just went in there and put on lipstick and fluffed up her hair.

Tommy had been educating Evan on Alabama football history for five minutes.

"Carla, they're talking football. Let's go get some champagne. The waiters never showed up."

As Carla led the way, she stopped every two minutes to hug someone or shake a hand. She's was quite vivacious for an accountant. Not my vision of a number-cruncher. I loved her very subtly sexy dress, and her handbag looked like a Judith Lieber. Very glamorous. I wondered how old she was.

It seemed to take five minutes to cross the big marble-floored ballroom with an overblown Rococo theme—velvet sofas everywhere. The drapes would make a perfect Scarlett dress. It was elbow to elbow.

"Whew! That took forever," I said as I joined Carla's side again.

"Sorry. I have certain people to kiss up to, and certain people I really like. They usually invite about a hundred and fifty, but I'd estimate there are more like two hundred people here tonight. I suspect they included certain prospective clients, as well as established ones. This is their official kick-off of the Christmas season, and it's always the first party on the social circuit. You haven't been here before?"

"No. Tommy just started doing business with them. With your firm." I took a champagne glass from a waiter who looked sixteen to me. He offered one to Carla.

"Only the best for the clients of Crandall, Lewis, Deaton & Hoffman. Cheers." She clicked my glass. "Lisa, are you a stay at home mom?"

"Yes. It's what I wanted to do since I had Delaney. I had big plans to go back to work when she was a month old, but the stay-home-hormones were overwhelming. I never expected to feel that way. I had a good job with IBM before she was born; Tommy and I both did. We left Atlanta after he got his airline software business up and running."

"You're not from the South, are you?"

It was more a statement than a question. Surely I was developing an accent by now.

"No. I'm originally from the Chicago area. IBM brought me to Atlanta. I loved Atlanta. I love Birmingham. I am learning to love living near Kudzu Corners, Alabama. You've heard of it, of course."

"You made that up."

"Okay, I did. Elfew, Alabama."

"You made that up."

"Nope. Google it. We have world-class bass fishing nearby." I grabbed another champagne. Carla shook her head no, thank you. "Delaney and Tommy love it there, and I love being with Delaney and Tommy. It really is beautiful, and peaceful. We have an incredible view from our house. Green pastures lead to the mountains in the distance. I have gotten very used to waking up to it. Tommy had a couple of acres of our land fenced in at the bottom of the hill, and he and his dad built a little corral. Delaney's getting a pony for Christmas."

"I grew up here in the city. My cousins had horses, and I was always jealous. Has Delaney had lessons?"

"Not for getting on a pony and being led around. I'm thinking of lessons for when she can ride the pony on her own. Do they have lessons for riding Shetland ponies? Shetland dressage? Tommy promised me a pony who will act like he's on tranquilizers. Either that, or I'll need tranquilizers."

Carla smiled and nodded her understanding.

"This house," I said, eying a massive chandelier, "is incredible."

"Isn't it? Junie Crandall grew up in it, you know. Old money. Steel money. Railroad money. Did you see her portrait? You could've glimpsed it down the hall back there; it hangs in the library. She's kneeling next to a huge white dog. About ten years old."

"No. You'll have to show me when the crowd thins out a little."

I wondered if Tommy was still talking to Carla's husband. An old man, hair gelled down slick on his head, walked by with a Playboy centerfold-like woman on his arm. She was wearing a gold sequined mini-dress and a huge white fur wrap. He strutted like a peacock in full display. I looked at Carla and raised my eyebrows, and we both giggled uncontrollably for a few seconds. "What was that?" I asked.

"That was Doctor Herbert Randolph the third, accompanied by floozy the thirty-third. He's quite the catch."

"Apparently. Oh. My. Gosh. Quick, come with me. Please." I pulled on Carla's arm, trying to drag her behind a group of chatting old ladies. "I can't believe he's here."

"Who? What man? Where?"

I grabbed another champagne and took a gulp.

The waiter gave me a knowing grin and maybe a leer.

"That man. Dr. Robert Clarke."

"You know Dr. Clarke?"

"Yes. Do you? Is he your client?"

"No. He's Bill Deaton's client. He never comes to this party."

Rob, 8:56 – 9:10

It was embarrassing, getting here this late, but it was my first

and last appearance at the Crandalls'. When I called to tell Bill I was
selling the practice and moving back to Tahoe, he insisted I come by
and have a glass of eggnog before leaving town. He had been very
good to me, and I was counting on him to handle a lot of tax
paperwork here in Birmingham for me. An older couple
approached me.

"Dr. Clarke, we're so happy you could come tonight. I'm Junie
Crandall, and this is my husband, Doug. Welcome."

How did she know my name?

"Thank you, Mrs. Crandall. You have a lovely home."

"Thank you very much. We enjoy it. We heard you're going to be
leaving us soon. Is that right?"

"Yes, I'm moving back to Nevada. I'm from Lake Tahoe. Last
Friday was our final day in the office, and I'm flying out a week
from tomorrow. I have to tell you, Bill Deaton has been a
tremendous help to me."

"Bill says very nice things about you. Please have some
champagne or eggnog. There are soft drinks in the drawing room if
you prefer." She smiled. Someone did an absolutely perfect facelift
on this lady. Flawless. Natural.

"I will, Mrs. Crandall. Thank you." Mr. Crandall and I shook
hands again, and they headed back into the crowd.

I scanned the room, looking for patients—an old habit. Some
women wanted me to recognize them in public; some wanted me to
act like we'd never met. I could be either a rock star or a pariah,
depending on the crowd. I probably knew some of these people, but
I didn't recognize anyone.

I took a glass of eggnog from a passing waiter and sipped. I
wondered where Bill was. I didn't want to have to stay too long.

And there she was, far away, but looking right at me. Oh, my
God. She looked so much like Jilly. My wife had been gone for
years, but as I caught Carla Hansen's eyes, I was fascinated to see
how familiar they were to me. Hers was one of the first eye
surgeries I ever performed, and I put a lot of artistry into my work. I

created those eyes. They were remarkably beautiful.

I knew she worked in the office, but I thought this was a party for just the partners and their clients. She quickly looked back at her friend, a stunning creature in green. Clearly, we would avoid each other. I walked into the room ahead, where it looked like most of the crowd was. Bill was probably in there.

I found him mid-sentence, telling some sort of football story to a group of men. He spotted me.

"Rob! Come on over here. I'm glad you came." He slapped my back. "This is Glenn, Les, Tom, and Earl. Boys, this is Dr. Rob Clarke. He's leaving our fair state for Nevada soon. Anyway, The Bear had them doing two a days, and it was July. Hotter than . . ."

I pretended to listen, but was peeking around Glenn to see if Carla and her friend had come in. I couldn't help it, I wanted a closer look.

". . . he set up trash barrels every ten yards . . ."

I wondered if anyone here ever tired of hearing about Bear Bryant.

There they were, approaching Carla's husband, most likely. Looked like it. The woman in green was Mrs. Robinson. I saw her months ago, and pretty much told her she'd benefit from blepharoplasty when the poor woman only came in to ask about Botox for some tiny wrinkles. I think she was insulted, and in hindsight, she probably had a right to be. I didn't think she even lived in Birmingham. What was she doing at this party?

". . . those boys were droppin' like flies, but Bear . . ."

She's looked over here, then looked away. Over and over. Not at me. No, at Tom. Definitely at Tom.

". . . he told me. I swear, that's the God's honest truth . . ."

She waved, a tiny, barely discernible below-the-waist finger wiggle, holding Tom's eyes. I saw him nod slightly.

"Bill, thank you so much. My wife and I have a long drive home, and we'd better get going. This was a great party." Tom shook Bill's hand, and received his farewell back slap. "Merry Christmas, Tom. Y'all come back next year."

As Tom crossed the room to his wife, Carla smiled brilliantly at me, then turned. It looked like they were leaving together.

"Anyway, The Bear calls him into his office, and he's shaking in his boots . . ."

It was about time for me to get going, too.

Steel

(Tom's Great-Great Grandfather's Sword)

I will tell you of my experiences; the ones remembered, the ones not spent in dark closets and attics and once, in a barn filled with hay. The things I whispered into the dreams of those who examined me, gingerly turning me over and over, as if I were fragile. I am anything but fragile.

I was forged in Prussia, white hot and then, cold blue. Thrust into the hands of a boy, a boy who wept at night; fat tears splashing. He did not want to go to war. I never heard his name.

Sheathed at the side of his horse; he used his gun, never me. When the horse collapsed, bleeding, the older boy grabbed me and ran. He sat in the tent hours later, running his finger back and forth along my blade, a gesture of love. "Look what I got," he bragged to his friends. I was his prize; the finest object he'd owned in his short life. He would not let them touch me.

This boy, the older one, was experienced. The first day, he ran me through the lung of a twenty-year-old private from Akron, Ohio. Pulled hard, tugging, to free me from the cold earth. Sliced another, older man nearly in two. Back in the tent, he told the others, "I

killed five Yankees." They were never men or boys. They were
Yankees. And, it was two. He killed two in that battle.

There were more and more in later days, though. The boy was
good; he had a feel for balancing my weight, the correct stance, the
right hold. He was fast, too. His name was Josiah.

We moved mostly at night, hooves flashing in the moonlight. The
boy was hungry. The boy was tired. He kept me close at hand; I was
his truest friend.

At Bentonville, he was shot in the arm, a searing pain that
brought him to his knees. He dropped me suddenly, but picked me
back up with his left hand, running as fast as he could. Always
running.

We went home to Hillabee, Alabama. By the time the boy's
infection cleared, the war was over. The boy was bitter. He was
secretly convinced he could have helped the South win if he had not
been hurt. Mostly, the boy was hungry, and he was so very tired. He
packed me away in a trunk, his ragged uniform on top. I was
moved to a barn, forgotten amid tools in the loft.

In 1916, Josiah was a very old man. He wore me at his side, in a
new hand-tooled leather sheath, to the Confederate Veterans'
Reunion in Birmingham. He told old-man stories, patting me with
pride in his trembling voice. He wept old-man tears. They pinned a
souvenir medal on his chest; took a photograph. Afterward, I went
back into the trunk, carefully placed by the hands of his wife. I was
left alone in an attic this time.

Many years later, I was removed with murderous intent, handled
for twenty minutes, turned over and over by an angry man. I was
moved to a small, dusty closet. The uniform, my constant
companion, was gone. I was forgotten again.

I was discovered a decade later by a sobbing woman. She
stopped crying and wiped the dust from the leather, curious. She
did not remove me from the sheath; she seemed afraid. I was
carried into the living room and placed on a table for her husband
to see. He pulled away the leather. He was excited. He told her, "I

think this was my great-grandfather's sword. My great-grandfather rode with Forrest." He was right on the first count. On the second, he was incorrect. He would never be able to find out for sure. It became the truth.

His name was Thomas. He took me to another house where I was stored away yet again, though wrapped in soft cotton. I was an object of pride, a treasure, a jewel in his hands. He showed me once, carefully cradled, to his young son. He told him of the Cause, "The war was not about slavery and its cruelty. My people were poor farmers who never owned human beings; they fought because they believed in their freedom. The war was about taxes and the right of each state to govern itself. The South was invaded by northerners who wanted to dominate our economy. And they sure did after the so-called Civil War." He said, in closing, "My great-great-grandfather fought with this sword at his side and served with the famous general, Nathan Bedford Forrest."

The little boy, wide-eyed, asked, "Was it ever used to kill people?"

Thomas said, "I don't know for sure, but I would expect so. This sword will belong to you someday." The boy nodded solemnly, touching my blade shyly, cautiously, before I was replaced in the cotton-lined box.

Thomas examined me on the kitchen table every Confederate Memorial Day, making sure there was no rust, no damage. He wondered what the war had been like. He tried to hear the cannons. He tried to imagine the killing, the pain. He tried to imagine how Josiah felt, so very young.

The boy, Tom, appeared next as a man of thirty-eight. I was cleaned and polished, hung over his mantel, gleaming in the firelight. That night, he called his son, Tommy, into the room. "What do you think what it was like, when your great-great-great-grandfather fought in the war? Could you imagine carrying this heavy thing from place to place, tired and cold and wet in the rain?

Your ancestor, Josiah Edward Robinson, was injured and had to come back early because he was unable to fight anymore. Josiah's place had a big white farmhouse and several pecan trees around it. My daddy, your grandfather, visited it when he was very young."

A crumbled chimney stands sentinel.

I was taken down occasionally; carefully, respectfully, slowly lowered into someone's waiting hands. They ran their fingers along, tentatively, lightly. Sometimes they wondered how sharp my blade really was, how many I killed, if they would have been man enough to fight in that terrible war.

All the while, I was whispering.

Pretty Is As Pretty Does

Ellen

It was Sarah Anne's seventieth birthday party, an event planned for months by her friend Ronald and attended by fifty of us, some from hundreds of miles away. I remembered as my mind wandered, picking at my red velvet cake and listening to her grandchildren read their glowing tributes.

"Gran is a very talented artist . . ." Jenny, her eldest granddaughter, offered from the podium.

Sarah Anne was my husband Tom's older sister; she lived in a lovely Victorian home. Behind it was an artist's studio that was a garage until the sculpture frenzy of 1968. Our son Tommy did prettier sculpture in his seventh grade art class than ever emerged from that studio. That was followed by the watercolor phase. Her paintings were soft and pretty. We had one hanging in our breakfast room, a mountain landscape in blues and greens. Then, a foray into cutting silhouettes, the kind you used to buy at county fairs.

"My grandma bakes the best oatmeal raisin cookies . . ." said her young grandson, Michael.

She was very excited about the Pillsbury Bake-Off in 1972. Sarah Anne worked for two months perfecting her blackberry apple pie.

She designed interesting pie crust decorations; some of them were flowers, some were tiny apples made of dough. She dusted them with red sugar.

"You have to make your entry stand out, Ellie. It's not enough for it to taste good."

She brought pie after pie to our house, and they were delicious. Late in the deluge, though, Tom and I swore off pies of any kind forever. Sarah Anne, in turn, swore off pie-baking after she didn't receive an award.

That experience led her to propose and produce our first big Junior League fundraiser, a cookbook called *Dessert: The Art of Dixie*. She had a committee of ten, but she did the majority of the work. I was on the committee, experiencing the force that was Sarah Anne in action. She got recipes from Fannie Flagg, Kate Jackson—who was famous at that time for *Dark Shadows*, not yet *Charlie's Angels*—and lots of local celebrities. It was a huge success. People cherished their copies of that book, last re-printed around 1982.

"She is very beautiful . . ." Lizzy, the tiny one said.

She had always been truly stunning. Sarah Anne never walked into a room without most eyes turning to admire her. When we were young, I was jealous of her; it didn't matter how hard I worked to put together the perfect outfit, hairdo and make-up, Sarah Anne could show up in some plain baggy dress and look like she stepped out of *Vogue*. She was beautiful in a Vivien Leigh/Delta Burke way, with huge green eyes and dark lashes. Her hair was once full and glossy, almost black, then white. She had a long-legged figure any forty-year-old would envy. She could turn a tablecloth into a chic ensemble.

"My grandmother always dresses pretty, and has the coolest old clothes," Lizzy continued.

She made jewelry—long, intricate beaded necklaces she learned to weave in a class at the Art Center. Eventually, there were matching bracelets and earrings. Then she started crafting clay beads with Chinese characters on them, but never showed any to a soul, as far as I knew. That led to Chinese brush painting.

"You will find her listening to classical music . . ." said Jeffrey, her cutest one.

Sarah Anne fell in love with Mozart in 1975, with every note of music he wrote, and read everything she could get her hands on about the man and his life. She installed an elaborate stereo system in the studio, with four big speakers, and she would sit for hours out there, listening. She moved on to other classical music later, but Mozart was always her favorite. I remember a brief flirtation with opera; she never fully embraced it.

". . . and brought Shakespeare to our town . . ." Jeffrey added.

Sarah Anne helped organize the first Alabama Shakespeare Festival in 1972. She was one of those who pushed for it, helped find funding, and made it happen that first summer.

"Everyone loves her." Jeffrey concluded.

Richard was her husband; an odd, quiet man. We never really understood that match, because he was the ice to her fire—the rain to her parade. He was a chemist, and invented an additive for gasoline. I don't know what it was, but it made him a huge success. He traveled, away from home for weeks at a time, Sarah Anne increasingly cheerful in his absence and irritable when he came back. They stayed together, miserable, for many years because of their daughters. In 1979, they divorced. Her settlement left her well off.

An oil painting experiment followed; it kept her in the studio for hours on end. We stopped ringing the doorbell out front during that period, sure to find her if we walked around back, feverishly applying paint to canvas. Tom said the oil paintings looked like they had a skin disease. I think she was trying to layer colors for effect, but the effect was weird and ugly. At the time, Sarah Anne thought she was doing something *avant garde*; later, she hated those paintings.

Her eldest granddaughter took the podium again. "She is always cheerful and happy . . ."

In 1980 she began her novel *Pretty Is As Pretty Does*. It was the story of a Louisiana woman who moved to New York City; I got confused about where it went from there. There were many re-writes. She told us that a friend in Birmingham had great plans for her novel, and was going to get it published within the next year.

"Pretty is as pretty does" is a phrase every Southern woman of a certain age has heard a thousand times. Most of us repeat it to our own daughters and granddaughters. As girls we are also reminded in parting to "be sweet" as in, "I'll be back to pick you up from the party at three o'clock. Be sweet." This came with a kiss goodbye from your mother, admonishment and blessing.

After Sarah Anne announced that she was near to completing her book, she stopped calling us, and was never there when we tried to get her on the phone. Her girls were both in college, and Karen contacted us. When she talked to her mom, she thought she'd sounded strange.

"Would y'all please drive over and check on her?" she asked.

Tom went, and found her bleary-eyed in the dining room, surrounded by mountains of handwritten pages and dirty dishes.

She said, "I haven't slept in a week; I've been drinking coffee all night and trying to finish the damned book." Then she collapsed into tears, shaking all over and bewildering poor Tom. He drove to the drugstore, bought some Sominex, and gave her a little more than recommended. She conked out for almost twenty hours while he tried to make sense of the papers, placing them in a big cardboard box. He cleaned up the house and slept on the couch, checking on her occasionally. The following day, she was still crying, and didn't seem to be able to stop. Tom made her go to see Dr. Judge, who sent her to some psychiatrist in Birmingham.

She told us, "I'm fine, and you should quit worrying about me. I'm giving up on my novel; it was never meant to be."

She was fine. We went by there a lot, and found Sarah Anne looking and feeling good, sipping wine with her friend Ronald on

the back porch or heading out to see a play or movie. She began her
next phase, an exploration of various types of collage work. The
studio was full of scraps of everything you can think of—rusted old
nuts and bolts, pieces from Monopoly games, old magazines, lace,
birds' nests.

She dated here and there, and had plenty of admirers. Men
flocked to her like bees to honey. She never let any of them get too
close, though. She always went back to her friendship with Ronald,
who worshiped her beauty and style in a way only a gay man could.
He was sitting next to her now, dapper in a black suit with cravat,
holding her hand and beaming.

". . . but she has traveled all over the world . . ." Jenny continued.

She took a trip to Europe with Ronald after she tired of collages.
He was an antiques dealer, and they were ostensibly on a buying
trip. When she came home, she announced that she was going to
take up stained glass. She was inspired by the cathedrals in France.

Other than the occasional detour into needlepoint and the flower
arranging years, she was very faithful to stained glass. She did some
pretty pieces, including one she had made into a sidelight by her
front door. She gave us a lovely small window for our anniversary
one year; two white doves surrounded by deep blue, rose and
green. It was in our powder room.

"Her family means the world to her.," Jenny said.

Yes, it did. She spent two years researching the Robinson family's
genealogy, traveling to Montgomery a few times and to South
Carolina. It was she who discovered Tom's great-great-grandfather
Josiah Robinson's homeplace, way out in the middle of nowhere.
Tommy and his family lived fairly close to it. She tracked down
Josiah's service records from The War Between the States, and got
herself into the United Daughters of the Confederacy.

"Gran is very creative . . ." Caitlin, a cutie in pink tulle, remarked.

Boy, Caitlin, you've got that right. Tom always said Sarah Anne
was a genius, with ideas running around like wild horses in her

head which she tamed and turned into accomplishments while the rest of us were still saddling up.

We were a little worried when she told us she was writing again, a series of magazine articles on art projects. What else? She told us, "I'm very sure that magazines are going to publish some, maybe all, of them. I sent them to several." She had shown them to her friends, who thought they were very good. She was not exactly young at that point, and never had the first thing in print. Tom would drop in unexpected on his way home from work once or twice to see how Sarah Anne was doing. We met her and her then-boyfriend Ken for dinner a few times. Sarah Anne seemed fine, except she was very excited about her magazine fame, something we were positive was not going to happen. We feared the let-down.

"I want to be a writer, like her, when I grow up . . ." Caitlin continued.

Within three months, though, Sarah Anne was on our doorstep, grinning from ear to ear, with a copy of her first piece in *Stitchery*. It was a how-to on needlepoint pillow construction, and had a picture of a pillow that was forever installed on her living room sofa. They paid her fifteen dollars. Eventually, more articles appeared in *Blank Canvas* and *Glassworks*. She even contributed to a textbook used in college art classes.

She wrote for fun, though she would have rather made wind chimes from sea glass. Or crocheted. Or sketched in charcoal.

Amazing, beautiful, fascinating Sarah Anne. Everyone loved her.

Starlight

Delaney—2008

I liked Michael okay, but he thought he knew everything. He was almost seven, so he tried to boss me around. He brought his cars over, and kept running them up and down the walls of my bedroom. I told him, "Grandma Ellen wouldn't like that," but he would not stop.

His sister Caitlin was even worse. She was thirteen, and was watching us. She spent her time on her cell phone. Every once in awhile, she came in the bedroom to yell at us, "Be quiet!" She flipped her hair around and rolled her eyes at us.

We were at Grandma Ellen's. Caitlin was supposed to feed us lunch, but she didn't. All she did was scream, "Y'all hush!" and slam my door closed. Michael said his dad says she is hormonal, but we don't know what that is. I think it means she is stupid and mean.

Mommy and Daddy went with Grandma and Granddaddy to a visiting. They would be back before supper. I hoped Caitlin fed us before then. My doll, Bunantha, was hungry, too. Michael kept trying to run his cars over her, and tangled one up in her hair.

They are my cousins, but they were bossy and sometimes they whispered secrets and didn't tell me. I was five, and no one told me anything. They came to see my pony, Buttercup. Caitlin petted her and rubbed her nose, but I don't think Buttercup liked her.

Michael said I didn't know anything because I was not in school yet. I knew a lot of things, though. I knew the letters of the alphabet, and I could write some of them. I learned them from watching the E-O show a long time ago. Mommy called it something else, but it's the one where they spin a big wheel and guess a letter and it lights up and the lady turns it around Ding. They had E's and O's a lot. Mommy was teaching me how to read, and I knew a lot of words. We made up rhymes, too. My favorite was, "A cat sat on a mat and ate a fat bat." I knew ballet up to fifth position. I knew how to ride my pony. I was going to kindergarten soon, too.

Michael said, "Let's talk about stuff. You have a pony and a dog. I have two dogs, a hamster, a snake and a cat." Michael loved to talk about stuff. "And, I have a PS2 and an X-Box 360 and I'm gonna get a Wii. You don't even have any video games, do you?"

He didn't stop for me to answer.

"I have an uncle who is a real baseball player. He plays for the Montgomery Biscuits. He's famous. You don't know anybody famous."

No, I didn't. I tried telling Michael about Mama D, but he didn't know her and didn't care. He said, "I have my own great-grandmother, and she is very old and she smells bad."

Caitlin poked her head in. She said, "I am going out in the backyard with Annie." That is Granddaddy's dog.

I told her, "I am hungry," and she said, "Go get cookies from the kitchen."

That was fine with me, but she should have been feeding us lunch. I bet Annie didn't like her either.

Michael took the cookie jar and set it on Grandma's table.

Chocolate chip. Michael was a hog, and ate way more than I did. He had a big glob of chocolate on his chin, and I did not tell him.

After he puts the cookies away, we decided to go catch flies. Grandma had these little birds with wings that open and close, and they were lined up under the big window in the living room. If we could catch a fly, we put him in there. Once, we had two in the biggest bird. It was fun. It was Michael's turn first, so I had to stand with the screen door open while he caught some flies and tried to make them come inside. He ran back in and around the living room, screaming like an idiot, because there were no grown-ups to hear. He said, "Two flies came in," but I didn't see them. We kept trying to find some outside and inside, but we gave up.

Michael said, "It is a bad fly day, because it has not rained lately. We have to try later, because it is too hot outside for flies."

I went upstairs to put Bunantha down for her nap, and to color, when Caitlin came back.

She tells us, "Wash your hands, because I'm making turkey sandwiches."

I asked her, "Will you cut the crust off of mine?" but I knew I would have to pull it off myself. I was not washing my hands for her. While she was cooking sandwiches, I got Bunantha and put her in the chair next to me.

Michael said, "That is stupid."

After lunch, Caitlin said, "You two have to take a nap," even though I was not a baby and neither was Michael. Michael and I both thought that was stupid, but Caitlin kept yelling, and it was easier to go upstairs and pretend to do what she wanted. She talked on her cell phone while she thought we were asleep, and finished painting her toenails black. She thought she was so grown up. She picked Bunantha up by the foot and carried her. I grabbed her and held her the right way, with her head on my shoulder.

Michael opened the window in my room after Caitlin went

downstairs, and let his cars run down the side of the roof until they dropped off and crashed down to the ground. When he got done with that, he colored in my book, making Barbie green and purple and drawing a beard on her. I was going to tell Mommy when she came back. On my bed I held Bunantha close so he couldn't bother her. I closed her eyes, and then mine.

When I woke up, Michael had found my dress-up box in the closet, and he was laughing really loudly at himself in the mirror.

"Look at me, Delaney. I'm Caitlin." He had on a fancy top with sparkles on it, and a feather boa Grandma put in there. He was twirling around, and then he acted like he was Caitlin. "Y'aaall huuuuuuuuush."

He swung his wrist up and down, and rolled his eyes. "Hey," he said, "Let's go put clothes on Annie!" His eyes were really wide, and I couldn't talk him out of doing it. Besides, it sounded fun.

Michael said, "Carry things that button, so we can get them on her."

Annie was snoring on her bed in the living room. We didn't see Caitlin anywhere. We rolled Annie over, which was hard because she was fat. She didn't fight with us, though. When she was lying on her back, I slipped her front paw into one armhole. Then Michael pushed her over toward me. Annie sneezed and yawned. It took forever to get her to stand up. Then I put her other paw in the armhole while Michael made sure the first side stayed on. It took a lot of tries, but we finally got Annie into a red top with ruffles around her neck. We buttoned up the back. It was too big, so I ran upstairs while Michael held her and got a scarf to tie around her belly. Annie tried to push the outfit off with her leg, and then to bite it off with her teeth. It was funny. Michael was rolling around on the floor, holding his stomach, laughing hard. But after awhile, I didn't want Annie to bite a hole in the top, so we pushed her down and undressed her. Next we tried a beautiful pink dress, but it didn't button, and we had to give up. I decided Annie needed jewelry, and that was very easy. She walked away toward the kitchen wearing pearls and a stretchy rhinestone bracelet way up on one leg.

"Oh, Annie, you are soooooo pretty," I yelled to her.

Michael said, "Crap!" which was a bad word. He picked up all the clothes, and yelled at me, "Get that stuff off Annie!"

I chased after her and pulled the jewelry off. Then I heard the car doors closing out front. Michael and I ran upstairs, carrying everything but a scarf I saw, still laying next to the couch. We shoved it all into my dress-up box.

"Whew." We shook our heads.

I ran to my mommy, but stopped at the top of the stairs because something was wrong. I hid behind the wall, trying to hear.

". . . will never be the same. It will take a long, long time for her to get over this. If she ever does," my daddy said.

Who was he talking about? Was he talking about me?

"She won't get over it, honey. But maybe she can learn to live with it," my mommy said.

I peeked around the corner. Grandma Ellen was crying, and Granddaddy was holding her. Her head was on his shoulder. My Aunt Sarah Anne, Michael's grandmother, was standing next to them, patting Granddaddy's back. Michael's mom and dad came in the screen door and closed the big door behind them. They seemed fine.

Michael sat down next to me, and I held my finger up to my lips. "Shhh."

"What?" he whispered.

I shrugged my shoulders. "My grandma is crying," I whispered back.

Mommy said, "I am so sorry she had to find him. They said it was there since he was born. I have never heard of such a thing."

Grandma Ellen was saying something to Granddaddy, but I

couldn't hear. They went toward the kitchen.

Michael looked at me. "Of course she's crying, stupid. They went to a funeral."

"What do you mean?"

"I mean, somebody died and they buried him. Don't you know anything?"

I heard my mommy. "I'm going to look for Delaney." But she didn't have to look for me, because I was running down the stairs to meet her. She picked me up and hugged me, even though I was too big for that. "Hey, Pumpkin, did you have fun with Michael? What did you do while we were gone?" Mommy had been crying, too. Her eyes were red and puffy, but she was smiling.

"We didn't do anything. Just played a little."

Mommy didn't put me down; instead, she carried me to the couch and hugged me. She was crying again. I looked up, but she had wiped the tears away. Knowing that my mommy was this sad made me feel tiny, and I curled up tight in her lap and patted her arm. She rocked a little, back and forth, holding me tight. I pushed away enough to look at her eyes and I patted her cheek, very softly. Then, she bit her lip and started crying again, wiping the tears away with the back of her hand.

"I'm sorry, Delaney. I'm fine, baby." She smiled at me, because she knew it scared me to see her like this. I put my head under her chin.

Caitlin came down the stairs. She had been in Grandma and Granddaddy's room. What was she doing in there? She smiled and made a little wave at us.

Mommy thanked her for watching me.

"No problem. We had lots of fun. Delaney is an angel, aren't you, sugarpie?" She leaned over, hands on her knees, to pat my head. "I tried to get her to take a nap, but I don't know if she ever fell asleep. They were pretty wound up. Bless her heart, she's probably tired."

I rolled my eyes at her. She walked off to the dining room where everyone was sitting. She passed my Aunt Sarah Anne coming into the room.

She asked, "Lisa, do you she want a cup of coffee?"

Mommy said, "No, thank you."

Then she ran her fingers through my hair, with her gold charm bracelet brushing my head. Aunt Sarah Anne was really old, but she was very pretty. She was wearing black pants with a black jacket that tied in the front, like my robe. She had a huge rhinestone brooch pinned on, the exact kind Mama D wore. I knew about jewelry, too.

"Hello, Delaney Wonderful Robinson, how are you?" she asked, sipping her coffee. That was not my name, and she knew it. Delaney Anne Robinson, named after her in the middle.

I told her, "I am named after you, remember?"

She replied, "Yes, my middle name is Wonderful, too." Then she put her coffee down, and took off her gold charm bracelet. She brought it over and handed it to me. "Want to look at this for awhile?" She knew I loved her bracelet. It had a tiny deck of cards that spread out, a church you can open and look inside, a bicycle with wheels that move, a fish that wiggled, and my favorite, a horse with legs and a tail that swung. Those are just the ones that moved. There were some with real diamonds. I sat up straight in Mommy's lap to spread it out on mine.

Grandma Ellen and Granddaddy were getting ready to go up the steps. I could hear part of what Granddaddy said, ". . . trying to keep him safe, Ellie."

Grandma said something back I couldn't hear. Her hand was on his back, like she pushed him up the stairs.

I looked at my mommy, wondering if she was going to cry again. She seemed fine. I opened up the church.

Michael plopped down at Aunt Sarah Anne's feet.

"Hey, handsome," she said, ruffling his hair.

Michael patted the floor, trying to get Annie to come over. Annie stared at him. I smiled at Michael, and he smiled at me, hoping we can dress her up again. That made me think of Bunantha. As soon as I was finished with the bracelet, I would have to get her.

"Hey Missy Prissy." I looked up and saw Daddy. "Will you go and get Bunantha? We need to leave in a minute."

I hopped up from Mommy's lap and gave Aunt Sarah Anne her bracelet back.

"Thank you," I said, "I love your bracelet."

She gave me a hug, and I ran upstairs.

Daddy told me, "Be quiet, because Grandma Ellen and Granddaddy are resting."

When I got back down, Daddy was carrying a pan covered in foil.

"Mom made an extra chicken casserole when she cooked Lily's. She wants us to drop this off at Mama's. Do you mind?"

Mommy said, "I don't mind," and then we hugged and kissed everybody goodbye. Except Grandma and Granddaddy and Caitlin.

After we drove away, I asked Mommy, "What is a funeral?"

Mommy turned around to talk to me and said, "It's a special time to remember someone who has died. You know what that means, like when Bud the Goldfish died."

I said, "When we flushed him down the toilet?"

"Yes, when he wasn't swimming anymore."

"Michael says they buried someone. What does that mean?"

"You have seen cemeteries, honey. They put people there after they die."

"I thought cemeteries were where they put your little statue when you die. They put people there?"

"When someone dies, their body is what's left after they go to Heaven. And yes, they put their bodies there."

Mommy keeps looking over at Daddy before she answers.

"Did I know the person that died?" I asked.

"You had met him, honey, yes. You might remember him from when we went to see Lily out in the country. His name was Daniel."

I thought a minute. "Daniel who had Legos? With his dog Rocket?"

"Yes, that Daniel."

He was so nice to me. He even gave me some Legos. No wonder everyone was crying. I felt like crying too.

"Why did he die, Mommy?"

"He had something that went very wrong in his brain. It's very rare and could never happen to you or me or Daddy. It was a strange thing. A sad, awful thing."

"His mommy and daddy must be very sad."

"Yes, they are, Delaney." Mommy turned around front and looked out the window.

"Did something hit him on his brain?"

"Nothing like that. It was a thing called an in-your-ism. It happened very fast. Like I said, it is something that could never happen to you."

I stopped asking questions after that. I didn't think Mommy wanted to talk about it any more. Besides, we were almost to Mama D's.

When Daddy unfastened me, I ran to the door. Mama D got there very fast. She hugged me and then held my face in her hands, kissing my head on top.

"Hello, darlin'," she said. Then she hugged Mommy and Daddy. We went inside and sat at her kitchen table.

"Are you hungry, Delaney?" she asked.

"Yes, ma'am."

"Would y'all like some of this casserole?"

Mommy and Daddy said, "No." They were full, but I was not. And I like Grandma Ellen's chicken casserole.

Mama D put some in the microwave, and turned around to talk to Daddy. "I am so sorry, Tommy."

Daddy took a deep breath and said, "It's awful for Lily and Millard. They tried so hard to protect him. He was volunteering at the fire department. He was happy there. And then . . ."

"I know, honey." Mama D hugged Daddy.

The microwave dinged, and Mama D handed me a plate and a fork. "Be careful. It might be too hot." She sat down and reached over, stroking my hair back away from my face. "Where is Bunantha?" she asked.

"Oh, no! She is in the car. I have to go get her." For some reason, it made me cry.

Daddy got up. "I'll go get her, Delaney."

Mama D said, "I'll walk outside for a minute with your Daddy."

Mommy yawned and smiled at me. "It's been a long day, hasn't it, baby? It's already dark. We need to get you home soon."

When Daddy handed Bunantha to me, I hugged her and let her sit in my lap while I finished supper.

Mama D wanted to know, "Would you like ice cream?" but I was too full.

Then she said, "Delaney, I want to show you something. Come here a minute." She walked off into her bedroom, and Bunantha and I followed her. She told me, "Climb up on my bed," and I let Bunantha lie down on the pillows.

Mama D came out with one of her big boxes of jewelry, full of her old rhinestone necklaces and bracelets pinned to black boards. We loved to look at them. "Delaney, I want you to do something for me. I want you to tell me things you know about Daniel."

"Well . . . he was very nice," I said.

Mama D said, "Okay, now select a bracelet or necklace for that, for Daniel being nice." So I picked a very beautiful big blue one that had extra sparkle, and Mama D took it off and put it on the bed next to me. "Tell me something else about Daniel."

"He loved Legos." Mama D pointed at the board, and told me, "Pick another one, for 'Daniel loved Legos'." I chose a clear necklace that looked like diamonds. She put that one beside me, too.

"Something else."

"He loved his mommy and daddy very much." She pointed at the board. I picked another bracelet, a yellow one full of rainbows. She put that in the pile.

"One more."

"Um. He had a dog named Rocket and he liked ice cream." This time, I decided on a wide choker of shiny crystal beads that Mama D wore a lot. The pile was getting big. It was beautiful, like in a treasure chest in a movie.

"Okay. Let's let Bunantha rest here for a few minutes. You come with me, and help me carry the jewelry."

We walked out to the little patio where she grew her plants. Mama D turned the big light on, then flipped a switch that made a bunch of tiny white lights come on in the trees around us. I looked up at her and smiled.

"Do you like it? Your daddy put those in there for me. Come sit down at the table over here." She grabbed a flowerpot and put it in front of us. "Let's put the jewelry in here." We piled it in, all of it sparkling so pretty in the lights, until it disappeared inside. "Let's say that this flowerpot is Daniel." She walked it a little bit on the table.

"That's silly."

"If I break this flowerpot, all of the beautiful things about Daniel are still there, right? He loved his mommy and daddy, he was very nice, he loved Legos, he had a dog named Rocket, he loved ice cream...those are the things that are really Daniel. Not his body. It's what's inside that's you. Outside is your flowerpot." She smiled. "So, Daniel's body isn't working anymore, and he doesn't need it," she dumped the jewelry into her hand, and put the flowerpot on the ground, "and this is the Daniel who went to Heaven to be with God."

"Where is Heaven?"

"Some people think it's in the sky. I'm not sure. I like to think it is, because you can see all those beautiful stars up there." She and I looked up, and it sparkled like diamonds.

"What is Heaven like?"

She smiled. "Lots of people have different ideas. I can only tell you what I think. You stayed at your Grandma Ellen's house today, right?"

I nodded.

"Even though your mommy and daddy weren't right there, you were fine because you knew they were coming to get you. And when they did, I bet your mommy gave you a long hug."

I nodded again.

"How did that feel? Was it happy and warm, safe and loved?"

"Yes. She hugged me a long time."

"That's what I think Heaven is like. Like a hug from God, welcoming us to him, that is more wonderful than anything you and I can think of."

"Do you think God is hugging Daniel?"

"Yes, I absolutely think God is hugging Daniel. And I think he is happier than any of us here on Earth can imagine. Even though we're really sad that we may not see him here anymore, he is here. The beautiful things about Daniel are here in our hearts forever." She smiled and put the twinkly jewelry in my hands, and we looked at it, and then up at the stars.

Made in the USA
Columbia, SC
11 October 2020